HEARTLESS GOON

Lock Down Publications and Ca$h
Presents
HEARTLESS GOON
A Novel by *GHOST*

Lock Down Publications
P.O. Box 870494
Mesquite, Tx 75187

Visit our website @
www.lockdownpublications.com

First Edition September 2019
Printed in the United States of America

This is a work of fiction. Names, characters, places, and incidents either are products of the author's imagination or are used fictitiously. Any similarity to actual events or locales or persons, living or dead, is entirely coincidental.

Lock Down Publications
Like our page on Facebook: Lock Down Publications @
www.facebook.com/lockdownpublications.ldp
Cover design and layout by: **Dynasty Cover Me**
Book interior design by: **Shawn Walker**
Edited by: **Lashonda Johnson**

Stay Connected with Us!

Text **LOCKDOWN** to 22828 to stay up-to-date with new releases, sneak peaks, contests and more...

Thank you.

Submission Guideline.

Submit the first three chapters of your completed manuscript to ldpsubmissions@gmail.com, subject line: Your book's title. The manuscript must be in a .doc file and sent as an attachment. Document should be in Times New Roman, double spaced and in size 12 font. Also, provide your synopsis and full contact information. If sending multiple submissions, they must each be in a separate email.

Have a story but no way to send it electronically? You can still submit to LDP/Ca$h Presents. Send in the first three chapters, written or typed, of your completed manuscript to:

LDP: Submissions Dept
Po Box 870494
Mesquite, Tx 75187

DO NOT send original manuscript. Must be a duplicate.

Provide your synopsis and a cover letter containing your full contact information.

Thanks for considering LDP and Ca$h Presents.

Dedications:

First of all, this book is dedicated to my baby 3/10, the love of my life and purpose for everything I do. As long as I'm alive, you'll never want nor NEED for anything. We done went from flipping birds to flipping books. The best is yet to come.

To LDP'S CEO- Ca$h & COO- Shawn:

I would like to thank you guys for this opportunity. The wisdom, motivation, and encouragement that I've received from you two, is greatly appreciated.

The grind is real. The loyalty in this family is real. I'm riding with LDP 'til the wheels fall off.

THE GAME IS OURS !

Judge not lest ye be judged bible
Matthew 7:1

And quite frankly, I DON'T GIVE A
FUCK!

I GOT THE STREETS !

Chapter 1
JaMichael

Lightening cut zigzags into the night sky with thunderous boom sending its warning sixty seconds later. From my position on the couch, I could hear the muffled sounds of my Auntie Veronica, and her husband Victor arguing about the bills of the household. It was approximately forty degrees outside, and the gas and electricity had been turned off for almost a week. The inside of the house was freezing. I sat there on the couch dressed in my black Bomber jacket, with mittens on my hands. I was both cold and hungry.

Victor had been missing in action prior to this day for almost four days. After he and Veronica were finished arguing about the past due bills, I was sure the topic of his absence would come up next. Them arguing and going at each other's throats seemed like a normal thing. It had been this way ever since me and my sister, Jahliya came to stay with Veronica after our mother was killed, and our father was sent to prison for the murder of my mother, and sisters. I didn't know if he was guilty of either, I was only a baby when the events took place.

Since I wasn't old enough to know anything, I'd always gotten the impression from those that knew my father, Taurus that he was a good man with a weakness for women. A man that would never physically put his hands on a woman and bend over backward for those he cared about. Even though I'd heard all of these great things, no one had ever taken the time to introduce me properly to my father. I was seventeen and six months old now and looking forward to turning eighteen so I could visit my pops on my own. I'd take my sister along with me. Even though she was older than me by four years we had yet to sit down in front of the man that helped create us. She said, she would wait until my eighteenth birthday before she did so.

The candle that was set in front of me on the table seemed as if it was seconds from going out. The candle had just about melted all the way leaving just a speck of wick. I leaned forward and blew out the flame and immediately the living room became dark. The scent of the burnt wax drifted to my nose, along with that of the wick. I sat back and lowered my head as the argument continued to go on.

Jahliya sauntered into the living room with a blanket wrapped around her body. Lightening from the night sky, revealed that she wore a pair of tight Capri pants, over thick wool socks. Her naturally curly hair was pulled back into a ponytail.

"Man, I hate this house. It's always so fuckin' cold in here." She plopped down on the couch next to me. I placed my arm around her body and held her. She rested her head on my shoulder. "JaMichael, I just gave auntie three hundred dollars. I wonder what she did with it?"

"I don't know, sis, but don't you think it's time we move up out of her crib?" I asked, holding Jahliya closer to me so I could absorb some of her heat.

"How the hell we gon' do that? I ain't got no money put up, and they ain't paying me nothing but minimum wage down at the Cleaners. Apartments might as well cost a million dollars because we can't afford that shit." She shook her head in defeat and sighed. "What about you? Have you gotten any luck on catching a gig yet?"

"Nah, I don' put in applications all over town though. Hopefully, somebody'll be calling me back soon. If not, I don't know what I'm finna do." It felt like it had gotten a few degrees cooler. My nose was ice cold, I was so tired of struggling. Damn, I was sick of it.

"Man, if ain't nobody trying to hit you with no job you might have to get down with, Mike-Mike. Daviah told me that her brother comes in the house every day with no less than five hundred dollars. Do you know what we could do if you brought home five hundred dollars a day?"

I laughed. "Hell yeah, first thing we could do is get this heat turned on. Probably be able to have a hot bath after not having one for so many weeks." I could imagine myself coming up with five hundred a day. For me, that was life-altering money. That shit sounded better than a steak dinner at the Outback.

"Mmm-hmm, that lil' scratch a get us right, lil' brother. We wouldn't need to stay at auntie's house no more. I could get us a place, and it could be just me and you. Peace and quiet for once. We could furnish the place, just hook it up and all that good shit, and just be alone. I'd probably make yo' lil' ass hold me all day long and couldn't nobody say nothing about it because they wouldn't be in our shit. You know what I'm saying." She lifted her head up, kissed my cheek and rubbed her nose against mine, then laid back with her head on my shoulder.

I didn't love nobody in the world as much as I loved my sister Jahliya. She was all I felt I really had. The only person I knew would have my back no matter what. Ever since our parents had left, she'd basically taken care of me as if she was my mother. I would die for Jahliya in a heartbeat. Even though I had never killed anybody before, I knew I would kill anybody over her. She was my life.

"If you want me, too, I can holla at, Daviah to see if she can hook you up with, Mike-Mike."

"I'm pretty sure she wouldn't have any problem doing that. Mike-Mike should accept you with arms wide open." She snuggled closer to me. "JaMichael, you got that hustle shit in you anyway. Our father, Taurus, was a legend. At least that's what everybody says down here in Memphis. I wish I had enough heart to go and see him, but I just ain't ready. I love you, though." She kissed my cheek.

I didn't know the first thing about hustling. I'd been hearing for years how knee-deep into the Game my father Taurus had been, and as much as it made me proud to know he was a legend. It honestly spooked me because I didn't think I had that hustle shit in me like he did.

"Sis, let me sit back and see if one of these gigs gon' get back to me before we go that route. Let's give em like a week. If don't nobody hit auntie phone by then I ain't gon' have no other choice than to pick up that bag."

Jahliya nodded her head against my shoulder. "You damn right you ain't. I'ma still lay the groundwork just in case. Ain't nan one of the jobs finna pay you no hundred dollars a day no way. You ain't finna get nothing but minimum wage, and as you can see, we gon' need more than minimum wage around this piece."

Veronica's bedroom door swung open. She and Victor stormed out of it arguing at the top of their lungs. Victor waltzed into the living room. From the constant flashing of the lightning outside, I could see he was reaching for his jacket. He grabbed it and slipped into it. Veronica rushed him and tried her best to pull it off his arms.

"Where you think you finna go, huh? Nigga you just got back in this house. You ain't finna go nowhere." She yanked the coat from him and slung it to the floor.

Victor turned around and stepped into her face. His shadows danced along the walls. Illuminated by the many candles that were decorated around the living room.

"Bitch if you don't stop playing wit' me, I'ma stomp a mudhole in yo' ass. Now pick my fuckin' coat up off that floor and place it in my hands."

Veronica smacked her lips loud enough for everybody in the room to hear it. "Nigga please, you don' lost yo' fuckin' mind. I'll be dammed if I do anything of the such. If you want that coat picked up, you finna pick it up on your own." She stepped into his face. "But you don't need it because you ain't going no fuckin' where. I thought I made that perfectly clear."

Victor stood five-feet-ten-inches tall, he weighed every bit two hundred plus pounds. He was bald-headed, with a bit of a gut. The way his physique was set up it was easy to guess that back in the day he was physically fit. Veronica was five-feet-five-inches tall, and every bit of a hundred and forty pounds. She was light caramel with a gorgeous face and shoulder-length hair that she dyed once a week whether she was broke or not.

"Bitch if you don't pick up my jacket from this floor, I'm finna fuck you up in front of these kids. Now keep playin' wit' me."

Veronica looked into his eyes for a short while and sucked her teeth. She slightly nodded her head as if they were in understanding and bent over to pick up the coat. She made it seem like she was about to hand it to him, but instead, she lifted it all the way over her head and slammed it down to the ground.

"I wish you would put your hands on me, Victor. You do that shit and you finna be sadly mistaken."

Victor looked down at his jacket for a long time. I felt severely uncomfortable. I didn't know what he was about to do but I wasn't finna allow him to whop on my auntie if I could prevent it. He was a man and in my opinion, men weren't supposed to beat women, even though that seemed like the norm for most couples here in Memphis. Using blazing speed, he stuck out his arm and began choking Veronica. He walked her backward and slammed her into the wall.

"Bitch now you done, done it? Now you done broke the camel's back."

Veronica beat at his hands, making gurgling sounds. Her eyes were wide open. Constant wheezing came from her nose. He lifted her so high her feet were no longer on the ground. She gagged some more and scratched at his arms.

I jumped up, and Jahliya tried to grab me. I jerked away from her and rushed the pair. Then wrapped my arm around Victor's neck and pulled as hard as I could. "Get the fuck up off of my auntie nigga. What the fuck wrong with you?" I demanded to know.

He dropped her and spun around to face me. "Fuck you say to me, you lil' bitch ass nigga?"

"Don't be calling my brother out of his name. He ain't yo' muthafuckin' child, Victor. Get that shit straight, right now," Jahliya snapped with lethal temper.

Victor waved her off. "Man shut up bitch before I choke yo' ass out too."

Now I was superheated, I pushed his big ass as hard as I could. He flew backward into the wall and bounced off it like a basketball. Then he rushed me, picked me up in the air and slammed me on the glass table sending shards of glass everywhere it seemed. My head ricocheted off the carpet so hard I found myself dizzy, and nauseous. He bent to pick me back up when Jahliya came swinging haymakers at him. Through my blurred vision, I saw her fucking him up blow after blow.

14

Then Veronica jumped up and was on his ass too. Both women were giving him the bidness. Jahliya took a step back and jumped forward kicking him in the nuts. Victor hollered out in pain, and cuffed his genitals, before falling to his knees in agony.

"Yeah, talk that shit now, nigga. You thought it was sweet. You thought you was finna put yo' hands on my lil' brother and get away with it?" Jahliya tackled him and bit into his face. They rolled around on the floor before Veronica jumped in to help Jahliya.

I slowly made my way to my feet feeling dizzier than I ever had before in my life. I staggered a bit and caught my balance by the use of holding the wall for support. When I finally shook the jitters out of my brain, I gathered myself and pulled Veronica off Victor. She'd been pummeling him blow after blow.

"Chill, Auntie, that nigga don't want no more smoke."

Veronica was riled up. "Fuck him, I'm tired of him putting his hands on me. He don't own me. I am not his property." She tried to go at him again.

I blocked her and slung her to the couch. "Chill yo' ass out, don't get up."

She crossed her arms and mugged me angrily. "Damn you, Ghost!" My aunt had a habit of calling me the nickname that my father Taurus had given me when I was born. I'd come out of my mother hella pale and didn't gain my caramel color until I was three years old.

I ignored her and pulled Jahliya off him next. Jahliya had been punching him back to back. Her knuckles were bloodied and swollen. "Come on, sis, fuck that nigga. Look at him, he ain't even moving," I said lifting her into the air.

She kicked her legs wildly until I placed her on the couch next to Veronica. Both girls hugged each other.

I kneeled beside Victor and pushed his punk ass. "Get yo' ass up and get the fuck out my auntie shit before I let these queens loose on yo' ass again."

The shiesty part of me wanted to punch him in the side of the head to get my lick back from him slamming me in the table. But just by the candlelight alone, I could see that he was swollen in the face. The women had done a number on him, and I could tell they wanted to finish him off. My whole life I'd heard people tell Jahliya that she had a horrible temper like her mother Princess. I wasn't old enough to meet, Princess. But if her temper was anything like my sister's she musta been a handful for my father, Taurus. I could only imagine how they coexisted.

Victor slowly came to his knees and began to stand groaning with every movement. When he was standing firm on two feet, he staggered backward and fell to his ass once again with blood running from his nose.

He took his fingers and dabbed them into the blood that was coming out of his nostrils and looked them over. "Damn, y'all ain't have to do me like this." He glanced toward the couch.

I assumed to see Veronica's expression. She continued to hold Jahliya as if he wasn't even there. Finally, he made his way to his feet, and stumbled toward the door, unlocking it, and stepping onto the porch. I picked up his jacket and threw it in his face before slamming the door shut.

Veronica stood up from the couch and dusted off her nightgown. "Well, that's just that. I don't need no man that think he finna be putting his hands on me. He ain't helping me with none of these damn bills. Got shit turned off all around me. I can do better than that. I can do better than him. Y'all have a good night. Thank both of you for having

16

my back." She picked up one of the candles and made her way toward the back of the house.

As soon as she was gone, Jahliya got up and walked behind me. She ran her hands over my back very cautious. "Lil' bro' did he hurt you in anywhere?" She came around and stepped into my face.

I shook my head. "N'all that fool just caught me off guard, that's all." Were the words that came out of my mouth even though my back was killing me. I think I had landed wrong or something because my shit was pounding.

"Well good, I swear if you wouldn't have pulled me off him I was finna try to murder his ass. Don't nobody put their hands on my brother. Were all we got, straight up." She kissed my cheek and rested her small hands on chest. "Let's go to bed, we can clean this glass and shit up in the morning when we wake up." She took hold of my hand and led me to the room we shared.

Ghost

Chapter 2

I had this lil' female named Tamia that I was sorta sweet on. By sweet I mean she was like my lil' shorty or whatnot. We went to the same high school. She and I had writing class fourth period together, and on most projects, we worked together since our brains seemed to always connect and agree on most writing assignments. Tamia was five-feet-three inches tall, about one-hundred and twenty-five pounds. She was light caramel, with brown eyes, and hair that came just to the upper portion of her back. She kept her hair permed, and it always looked so silky, and shiny. She also had dimples that were as deep as mine that made me feel some type of way.

Two days after Jahliya and Veronica whooped Victor, Tamia waited for me after school, so I could walk her home. When I came out of the backdoor of the building she rushed over, handed me her books and kissed me on the cheek. It was about eighty-five degrees outside, and humid as hell. I was rocking a grey, white beater over Guess denim shorts that Jahliya had copped for me, over a pair of gray and black Nikes that had seen better days. My clothing options always made me feel so insecure because I didn't have much to choose from.

Tamia wrapped her arms around my neck and looked into my eyes. "Guess what, baby?"

"What's that?" The sun was so bright it was causing me to have a headache.

"My mother working both of her jobs tonight, you know, the second, and third shift. She ain't gon' be home until seven tomorrow morning."

I held her firmer around the waist. "And, why you telling me all of this?"

Behind us, people were loading onto their school buses and kissing their high school loves goodbye for the day.

She blushed. "Well, you already know why. I mean, I know I been kind of scared to do the most and everything, but now I think I'm really ready. Long as you promise to take it easy on me." She bit her lower lip and batted her lashes at me.

I laughed, I didn't know how to tell her that I really wasn't all that cold. I had only been with one female in my life. I hadn't done more than put it inside her, and pump back and forth before her parents came home causing me to jump out of the window.

"Yo', it's all good, baby. I promise to take it as slow as you need me too."

She smiled, stepped on her tippy toes and kissed me on the cheek again. "A'ight, that sound cool. Come on let's go." She took a hold of my hand, and sort of dragged me along.

The whole time I couldn't help but admire how her ass was jiggling all under her summer dress. The hem flirted just below her ass cheeks. Tamia was strapped even though she was a year younger than me. When we got halfway down the block to her house she had me wait while she ran ahead to make sure the coast was clear. While I was waiting under a tree to shield myself from the brutal sunlight, my teacher Mrs. Jamie pulled into the driveway of the house I was waiting in front of. Mrs. Jamie was my Creative Writing teacher. Before she pulled all the way up the driveway she stopped and rolled down the window of her Nissan Maxima.

"JaMichael, boy what are you doing on my block?" she asked, smiling.

I was caught off guard, I didn't want to get Tamia in trouble. So, I started to think of a lie, right away. "Uh, I'm just chilling," was all I could come up with.

She smirked. "You just chilling, huh? Well, why don't you chill over here and come talk to me." She waved me over.

I looked both ways before I stepped over to her car and rested my hands on the driver's window will. "What's up, Mrs. Jamie?"

Mrs. Jamie was dark-skinned, with brown eyes. She had a body that made most of the teenage dudes in our school nervous because she was so well put together. She was real thick down low, and slim up top. Even as I stood in front of her car, I was more nervous than a dude on trial for murder.

She licked her juicy lips. "I hope you ain't on my block causing no trouble. I'd hate to have to call your auntie and tell her that you're raising our crime rate over here."

The way she looked into my eyes made me feel some type of way. All of a sudden I started feeling super hot. "N'all, I'm just chilling waiting on a friend, that's all. You ain't gotta worry about me getting in no trouble." Sweat slid down the side of my face.

She looked me up and down. "A friend, huh? You wouldn't be talking about yo' lil' girlfriend Tamia, would you? Do her mama know what y'all be doing while she's at work?"

I wiped my sweat away and took a step back. "Mrs. Jamie, you tripping. We ain't on nothin' like that, we're just friends."

"Yeah, okay, and I was born yesterday." She laughed shortly. "Shouldn't you be headed off to work somewhere? That's what most of our seniors do after school."

"I been trying to find a job, but so far I ain't had no luck. I'm waiting on a few callbacks now." I looked over my shoulder to see if Tamia was on her way back from the house yet. The longer I talked with Mrs. Jamie the more nervous I became especially when she asked me to step back. She pulled the car the rest of the way up her driveway and got out and popped the trunk. The wind blew, forcing the fabric of her dress up against her plump ass. I felt my dick getting hard on sight.

"JaMichael, help me carry these grocery bags into the house." She grabbed three of them and made her way upstairs.

I was wondering how she had already managed to go shopping when they had just let school out. I grabbed the five remaining heavy bags and followed behind her. The scent of her perfume seemed to put me in a trance.

"Mrs. Jamie, how did you manage to buy all of this stuff already? School just let out," I said setting the bags on the table.

She placed her purse on the counter, just as her black Labrador slowly entered the kitchen. "Oh, Walmart allows you to order everything online now, and they have it ready for pick up when you get there. It's convenient." She rubbed the dog's head and pat her butt. The dog gingerly left out of the kitchen. She walked around the groceries and stepped in my face. "I make you nervous don't I, Ja-Michael?"

I swallowed hard and held my ground. My brain was screaming, '*Hell yeah*!' "Nah! Why would you make me nervous?"

She stepped a bit closer and rubbed her nose from side to side against mine. She looked into my eyes and her perfume was louder. "Because I see how you look at those lil' girls that roam around the halls at school. Then I see how you look at me. Don't you know, I am a married woman, huh?" She placed her hand on my chest and rubbed down until it was resting right on my crotch. She squeezed my piece through my shorts and held it. "On top of that, I am your teacher, and old enough to be your mother."

I don't know why, but when she said those last two parts my dick got hard as a rock and throbbed in her hand. "Mrs. Jamie, I don't know what you're talking about. I ain't never came at you bogus."

She undid my belt and shocked the shit out of me when she reached into my boxers and took ahold of my pipe. Her thumb ran in circles around the head. It felt so good, I let out a noise that embarrassed me.

She sucked my neck. "JaMichael, I'm a grown-ass woman. Do you know what I would do to you?" Now she had my lil' young piece out stroking it.

I closed my eyes and held the table. "Damn, Mrs. Jamie, what would you do?"

Just then we heard her husband's car pulling into the driveway. She pulled her hand back and told me to hurry up and fix my stuff. My dick was so hard, it damn near made it impossible, but I did just in the nick of time. Montell came through the door and stopped in his tracks when he saw me. He was six feet and bald. Before he could say anything, Mrs. Jamie handed me a textbook and scooted me on my way.

She whispered in my ear as I was on the way out, "We'll finish this another time, baby."

****

Later that night, I sat across from Tamia while she took photos with her phone of all the answers from Mrs. Jamie's Teacher's edition textbook she had handed me, I guess, on accident. She'd been doing this for a full hour when I started to get irritated. Mrs. Jamie had me all riled up, I was trying to take my sexual frustrations out on Tamia.

"Damn, is this all we finna do?" I asked, allowing the irritation to be heard in my voice.

She snapped three more pages. "I still can't believe she just gave you her book like this. That woman must got a thing for your fine ass." She nodded her head to Moneybag Yo' coming out of her speakers.

"Man, did you hear what I asked you?" I was ready to get up and leave.

It was plenty of females in Orange Mound that wouldn't hesitate to buss down. In fact, I knew about a whole house full of females that got down with damn near every dude around our hood. I didn't know if they would mess with me, but I did know they threw parties every Friday. I was thinking about hitting it up and trying to get in where I fit it.

She placed her phone on the table and stood up in front of me in a pink tank top and black and pink Victoria Secret lace panties. The first thing I noticed was how much the crotch of the material was all up in her sex lips. I could see a hint of brown on each side; her kitty was fat. My piece stood at attention.

"Dang JaMichael, you know damn well I wouldn't call you over here if I didn't have something else on my mind. I'm just a lil' nervous. Can you tell me how I look?"

I ran my eyes over those thick thighs, up to her nipples that were sticking up against her shirt and had to take a deep breath. "Shorty, you fine as hell. Ain't nobody at school fuckin' in yo' bidness."

She smiled. "Okay, that gave me a little confidence, but I don't like when you call me, Shorty. Can you call me baby or boo? I just need things to be a lil' more endearing since I'm getting ready to give you my virginity." She stepped forward, took hold of my hand and placed it between her thighs. "Go on."

I shuddered, I wanted to hit that pussy so bad I woulda said anything. "Man, Boo, I think you crushing every girl at our school. Them hoes ain't got no other choice than to hate on you. When y'all be doing your cheerleading thing and all of that, I don't have my eyes on nobody other than you," I lied, rubbing all over her lil' pussy. It didn't take long before the fabric got a wet stain.

She spaced her thighs. "Unnhhh, JaMichael, is you just saying that, or are you serious?" Her eyes were lowered into slits. Her nipples were super hard now.

I scooted forward on the couch and sniffed her front. It smelled like perfume, with a hint of pussy. Now my piece was jumping up and down like crazy. "I ain't lied to you since we been fuckin' around. I ain't got no reason to. I got the baddest bitch in the school. Know that!" I slipped my fingers into her leg hole, and over her lips that had a light coat of hair on them.

Her slit was leaking, when I rubbed up and down in between her folds it felt slippery and hot. She moaned and placed her foot on the couch pillow to the left of me.

"Play wit' me, JaMichael. It feels so good, play wit' that lil' button at the top of my kitty." She took a step back, pulled her panties down, stepped out of them, and placed her foot back on the couch.

I placed my nose inches away from her gap and took a big whiff of her natural scents, the smell made me shiver. She opened herself up with two fingers and moaned deep within her throat. I started to play with her lil' slippery button. The more I played with it the wetter she got until it was oozing down her inner thigh. She sat down on the couch and spread her thighs wide.

"JaMichael, can you eat me like they be doing in my mama movies? Please! I talked to some girls in my class, and they said it would feel so good. They boyfriends do it to them before they get down." She started to play with herself.

I stood there on rock hard, thirsty. I wanted to fuck Tamia so bad it was irritating me, but I didn't know about putting my mouth down there. I started thinking back to a few weeks ago when she said we couldn't do nothing because she was on her period. I thought about blood coming out of where she wanted me to lick, and it made me nervous.

"I'm saying, Shorty, you're a virgin. My homie told me that it ain't smart to go down on a virgin before you hit. He said it makes the experience bad for them," I lied. Didn't nobody ever tell me that. I just wasn't trying to take that trip down south.

Tamia took her slick fingers out of her gap and rubbed them on her thick thighs. She left a trail of juice along the way. "You for real?"

"Hell, yeah. You just gotta let me get in there, then we can get on all of that freaky shit later. Now just lean back." I worked myself out of my shorts and stood before her in my boxers. My piece stuck through the hole in the middle of it. There I was stroking it until it swelled up like an angry brown cucumber. I don't think Tamia had ever seen me so aroused. Her eyes were bucked. She slowly started to shake her head.

"Bae, I don't think I'm ready. That looks like it's too much to fit in here."

I kneeled beside her on the couch and rubbed her pussy. "Baby, it's good, all you gotta do is trust me." I tried to slip a finger into her box, she tensed up, and knocked my hand away. I really got frustrated.

She sat up. "Baby, I'm sorry, but I ain't ready." Her head was lowered. She sighed. "Are you mad at me?"

Hell, yeah, I was. I was mad and annoyed as a muthafucka, but I knew I had to spare her feelings. I sat beside her on the couch with my fingers smelling like her sex.

"N'all, I'm good, I gotta respect you. If you're not ready, you're not ready. I gotta get out of here, though. I'm horny as hell." I started getting dressed.

"Wait, that don't mean you gotta leave. We can do something. We just can't go all the way," she bargained.

I shook my head, I was too irritated to be in her presence. "N'all, I gotta get back home, anyway. I told my auntie, Veronica, I was gon' help her move some furniture," I lied. I made sure I was straight, then headed for the door. When I got there Tamia rushed to block my path. "Shorty, get out of my way."

"Nope, you ain't finna do nothin' but go out there and fuck somebody else. I told you, we can do something else. We just can't go all the way." She looked desperate.

I stared her down for a few moments, then picked her lil' ass up and moved her out of my way, before kissing her on the cheek. "I'ma hit you up in the morning. We good so don't trip."

She kept calling my name as I made my way out of her mother's crib, ignoring her.

Chapter 3

When I got home that night, Jahliya was waiting up for me. She had candles lit all around the room to illuminate it. She stood up from the edge of the bed dressed in a T-shirt that stopped at the top of her thighs. She gave me a look that told me she was pissed off about something as her shadows spread across the walls.

"Let me guess, you was over there trying to get some from Tamia, huh?"

I came in, took my shirt off, and hung it on a hanger. Because my auntie only had three bedrooms, me and Jahliya were forced to share a room, but it didn't bother either of us because it had been that way ever since we'd come to stay with her. The third bedroom was reserved for my cousin Danyelle. Danyelle was Veronica's sixteen-year-old daughter. She spent half of her time with her father, and the other time with Veronica.

"You already know I was, but once again, she chickened out. That shit starting to get me irritated. I'm about ready to drop her ass." I took off my shorts, folded them and placed them on the floor beside the bed. Then grabbed my toothbrush and walked into the half bathroom that was connected to our room.

Jahliya came behind me and wrapped her arms around my body. She rested her chin in the crux of my neck. "Lil' bro I don't know why you keep sweating that bitch, anyway? She pretty, but she ain't all that."

I continued the routine of brushing my teeth. Spit the toothpaste into the sink and ran the water, gargling a bit of it. When I turned around Jahliya was looking into my eyes. "You know I love you, right?"

I nodded and held her lil' waist. "For sho' I do, I know that we're all we have in this world. It's always been that way." I hugged her to my body.

She emitted a moan as my arms enwrapped her. "Dang boy, I love when you be snatching me up, and hugging on me the way that you do. I can feel your muscles growing too." Her own arms wrapped around my neck. "I'll kill for you, JaMichael. If anyone of those bitches ever hurt you, I swear to God I'ma kill one of them? All you really need is me, I will never hurt you." She kissed my neck, then my cheek. She took a minor step back, stepped on her tippy tocs and kissed my lips, sucking the bottom into her mouth.

I held her and rubbed all over her back. I could feel that she didn't have a bra on, and as crazy as it sounds that excited me. Maybe it was because both Mrs. Jamie and Tamia had heated me up so much. I rubbed all over her back and continued to kiss her, while she tilted her hips forward. My pipe started to stretch.

She licked my top lip, and stood back, looking me over. "Dang, I hope you know I can feel how hard your dick is, right now? I know you bet not be getting aroused because of me."

I backed up and placed my hand in front of my crotch. "N'all, Tamia got me like this, I'm tired." I walked past her into the room and sat on the bed confused.

Jahliya had always kissed me before we laid down to go to sleep. I didn't understand why all of a sudden I was physically feeling some type of way now. I pulled my socks off and ran my hand over my waves. She came into the room and stood in front of me for a second, then she smiled as the candle lights reflected off her beautiful face. She pulled up her T-shirt, and straddled my lap, placing a thick thigh on either side of my body. She wrapped her arms back around my neck and looked into my eyes.

"That bitch ain't got nothing on me. Why you gotta lie?" she whispered.

"What are you talking about?" I asked, feeling her kiss on my neck. This was something she had never done before, it made me nervous.

"You know damn well, I made your thing hard because I can feel it under me, right now. Why you just can't admit that I turn you on? Damn, it ain't a big deal." She pushed me back and kissed all over my neck and chest. Then she licked my nipples and kissed her way down my abs until her lips brushed the waistband of my boxers, she kissed along it. My dick was already sticking straight up.

I wanted to make her get up, I wanted to tell her she was tripping. That she was my big sister, and we couldn't get down under no circumstances, but another part of me wanted to see how far she would go. I needed to see, I was fiending to know.

She stuck her hand in my boxers, grabbed my pole, squeezed it in her fist, and began pumping it. "You don't need that bitch, Tamia, bro. You got me, it ain't nothing in this world I wouldn't do for you." Her speed increased.

I laid on my back with my eyes closed while she worked me. When I opened them, I saw that her right shoulder strap had fallen down enough to show off her full breast. It jiggled up and down, the nipple was hard as a rock. The sight was too much for me. In a matter of ten seconds, I was cumming all over her fist, while she sucked my neck.

When she finished, I cleaned myself up, and we spooned. She helped me wrap my arm around her waist, while she scooted back into my lap. Her ass felt hot and soft. I knew we'd just crossed a serious line, but I didn't know what to do about it. I didn't know what to say or think, so I didn't say nothing at all, and neither did she.

****

The next morning was more silence. We squeezed past each other without saying a word as we got ready to leave the house, so I could meet up with Mike-Mike. For some reason, I felt incredibly shy and awkward around Jahliya now. I didn't know what was going through her mind. After we got dressed, we stood on the porch in the scorching heat and waited for Mike-Mike to pull up.

Jahliya finally broke the silence. "Look lil' bro, I hope you ain't salty at me for what we did last night? I don't feel like we did nothing wrong. I'm your older sister so I gotta make sure I take care of you at all times, I don't give a fuck what this world says. You understand me?"

I nodded. "Aw, n'all, I ain't feeling no type of way at all. I just didn't know what to say to you that's all."

She frowned. "You say the same shit you been saying, ain't nothing changed. But I will say this, I don't give a fuck what you do with those other hoes out there as long as you keep me first. Don't never let no nigga, or bitch come before me. Do you feel me?"

I nodded. "Yeah."

"If I wanna lay-up with you every night that's my right. We are one and don't nobody understand our bond. We been struggling together since we were babies. I'd never allow nobody to come before you. I belong to you first, and it should be vice versa." She kissed my cheek and stood back with a mug on her face.

"Look, sis, fuck this world, it's all about us. Like I said, I'm good. We gotta be there for each other no matter what. It's good." I hugged her and had visions of kissing her soft lips again. I didn't know what was going on with me.

Mike-Mike pulled up in a drop-top, cherry red Mustang, sitting on twenty-eight-inch Spinners. He stopped in front of the house and tapped his horn.

Jahliya looked down at him and smiled at me. "Look, bro, you need to connect with this nigga. If he can help get you put on in the Mound, we'll be good. Just let me carry the conversation and follow my lead."

"Cool, come on," I said, following her to the Mustang.

When we got there Jahliya stopped and looked at Mike-Mike as if he were crazy. "Nigga you better get yo' ass out of this car and come open my door. I don't know what the fuck you think this is?" she snapped.

Mike-Mike smacked his lips and hopped out of his whip. He was five-feet-ten-inches tall, dark-skinned, with neat dreads that fell down his back, they were dyed red on the tips. "Shawty, you lucky you as fine as you is. I don't be opening doors for hoes and shit," he said, pulling the door open for her.

I wanted to say something slick to this nigga for insinuating that my sister was a ho, but she gave me a look that said chill. "Nigga, lucky for you, you ain't dealing with no ho. I'm a Queen."

Mike-Mike sucked his teeth. "I don't know about all that. I mean you definitely fine as hell, though." He looked over at me. "What's good wit' you, homie?"

"I'm JaMichael, Jahliya my sister. She wants us to link up." I balled my fist and held it so he could give me dap.

He left me hanging and walked around the front of the car, eyeing Jahliya the whole time. He jumped into his whip and looked back at me. "Gon' jump in homeboy, let's rap for a minute."

I hopped inside and struggled to get comfortable. His seats were hot as hell. I felt like a chump after he snubbed me on the cap. I decided I didn't like Mike-Mike already. Plus, I wasn't cool with how he was eyeing Jahliya like she was a piece of meat.

He pulled away from the curb banging 21 Savage, his bass was knocking. He turned it down enough so we could hear him. "So, this is the brother you was talking about?"

"Yep, that's my heart back there. I need you to put him on. He got that hustle shit in his blood. Trust me you won't be sorry," Jahliya said promoting me as if I knew how to hustle.

In all honesty, I didn't know the first thing about doing none of that shit. I wasn't square but compared to the other young niggas in the hood that pushed packs on a daily basis, I might as well had been.

"Oh, yeah? Well if I put your brother on, where does that get me with you?" Mike-Mike wanted to know.

I could see him eyeing her caramel thighs hungrily. From my vantage point, I made out the fact that the hem was just below her crotch. He dared to squeeze her left thigh, then rubbed all over it inching her hem up. She and I made eye contact in the passenger's side rearview mirror. I was seething.

She smacked his hand hard and pushed it off her. "You got one hell of a hustler on your team, and I'll owe you one," she said continuing to look me in the eyes through the rearview mirror. I was the first to look off, I didn't know what she meant by owing him one but when I imagined that nigga on top of my sister it made me feel sick on the stomach.

Mike-Mike smiled and continued to drive. He looked over at her. "Man, Shawty, I swear I don't be sweating no women like I been sweating you. Usually, if a bitch ain't tryna fuck wit' me, I tell her ass to push on, but it's something 'bout you that I really like. I just can't put my finger on it."

"Well, if you put my brother on you might get the chance to put more than your finger on it." She eyed him seductively.

Once again, I found myself getting more and more heated. I didn't understand what was going on with me.

Mike-Mike looked into the backseat. "Say, Mane, what is your forte?"

"My what?" I asked looking at this fool like he was crazy.

"Your forte in these streets, homeboy? What have you moved before? I wanna make sure I put you in the right lane with something you're familiar with. Because if I plug you with my big homies and you fuck off their packs, I'ma have to take a good look at you. It's as simple as that."

Jahliya sucked her teeth. "Fuck you mean, you gon' have to take a good look at him? I know you ain't talking about putting your hands on my brother?" Her caramel face turned a shade of red.

Mike-Mike shrugged his shoulders. "N'all, it ain't even like that. But the way this shit goes is if I bring him to my big homies, and they plug him into the game, I'm gon' be responsible for everything he do. So, if he fucks up its equivalent to me fuckin' up. If he creates a mess, I'ma have to clean it up. That's how this game goes."

"Yeah, well, ain't nobody finna touch, my brother. He ain't gon' make no mistake because I'ma be right there by his side to make sure he don't. Secondly, I don't give a fuck who your big homies are if they ever think they gon' touch JaMichael, I swear to Jehovah, I'll kill every last one of them. Then I'd come for your ass. I pray y'all don't try me!" She turned her pretty face into a scowl and caught my eyes in the passenger's rearview mirror again.

Mike-Mike bent a corner and took the road leading to Washington Park. "Say, JaMichael, long as you do what you're supposed to do, you ain't gon' have to worry about nobody doing nothing to you. I just wanted to let it be known what would be expected if shit went off to left fields. You feel me?"

I nodded. "I can hold my own, bruh. Ain't nothin' stupid about me." I knew Jahliya had a habit of sticking up for me before I could ever get a word in edgewise, but I was far from slow, or sweet.

I felt like Jahliya was used to just sticking up for her kid brother because she had ever since we were basically toddlers. I appreciated my sister, and I would kill for her in a heartbeat.

"Well, that's what I like to hear." He pulled into a parking space inside of Washington Park.

It was already packed, it looked like there was a full-court game of basketball going on. There had to be at least thirty spectators on the sideline watching it. A short distance from the courts where a bunch of females barbecuing in short daisy dukes that showed off their voluptuous thighs and asses. They danced, and twerked to a song by Money Bagg, never losing their flow of cooking. There was a bunch of little kids running back and forth chasing each other with water guns. There was also a group of about eight girls jumping double-dutch and singing nursery rhymes.

Off in the far distance was four men sitting at a picnic table not far from the females that were barbecuing. There were a couple of angry-looking dudes standing close by them with their hands under their shirts. The dudes were constantly looking in all directions. I guessed these dudes were their security.

"Why you bring us here?" Jahliya asked surveying the area.

"Because, if I'ma put JaMichael on, I gotta introduce him to a few power players in the Mound. You see that picnic table over there, JaMichael?" He nodded his head in that direction.

"Yeah, I see it. What about it?" I turned my neck to get a better view.

"The two niggas sitting down talking on their cell-phones run the whole Orange Mound. The brown-skinned nigga with waves name is Phoenix. He's a good dude, and more susceptible to putting the lil' homies on and treating us right. He makes sure the whole Mound is eating. He's the one I really wanna introduce you to."

"And who is the dark-skinned nigga with the mug on his face?" Jahliya asked.

"That's my older cousin, Mikey. That muthafucka ain't got no good sense. He's the reason I was saying if your brother fucks up, shit was gon' get real hectic. Phoenix got patience, Mikey ain't got none."

"Damn, what y'all whole family's name got some kind of Michael in it?" she asked.

Mike-Mike shrugged his shoulders. "Damn near, but that ain't important. What's important is, JaMichael be on his game at all times. Those niggas run the Duffle Bag Cartel. If your brother can show that he's stomp down and loyal, they'll plug him into their brotherhood. In return, he'll stay flooded with cash, and pushing shit as slick as this. I'm finna go see if they'll meet him, right now. I'll be right back." Mike-Mike grabbed a red bandana from the glove compartment and hung it from the right side of his back pocket, before walking over toward the picnic table. Before he was able to approach them, he was patted down, and his gun was removed from him.

Jahliya exhaled loudly, shaking her head as she watched from a distance. "Damn, I can't believe it's come down to this, JaMichael. Why do life gotta be so fuckin' hard?"

I rested my hand on her shoulder. "It's good sis, I got this. Life ain't finna be that hard for much longer once things get to rolling. Sooner or later I gotta stand up and be a man anyway, right?"

"Yeah, but if them niggas hurt you, I swear to God, man—" She hung her head. "—I don't know what I'd do."

Mike-Mike jogged back to the car with a smile on his face. "Come on, Dawg, they wanna meet both of y'all."

Chapter 4

Phoenix placed his arm around my shoulders and insisted we take a short walk through the park. The whole time I noticed he had two of his security detail following us at a safe distance. I didn't know how I felt about this nigga having his arm draped across my shoulders like I was abroad or something, but I had to keep in mind what was at stake. The bills were piling up, me and Jahliya were broke as a joke, and Veronica seemed like she was at her wit's end. I had to make shit happen, I was the man of the house.

"So, tell me what your struggles are lil' homie, and be real?" Phoenix was close to six feet, brown-skinned, with a muscular build like myself. He carried himself with confidence and spoke just barely above a whisper.

"Right now, we sitting in the dark at home. The gas and electricity has been turned off. There is barely any food, and shit is looking like it's going to get worse before it gets any better. I'm the only man, I gotta make it happen for the women in my household." I didn't know him from Adam, but I felt comfortable confessing to him for some reason.

"Damn, bruh, that seems to be the case for most of the lil' homies around the Mound, and Black Haven for that matter. It's like the world done forgot about the hood." He shook his head and we settled at a picnic table in the middle of the park. "Have a seat lil' bruh, let me rap with you for a minute."

I sat on top of the table. We were sitting under a big tree, and there was a nice breeze coming from the East that felt so good amid the hot day. "I'm letting you know, right now, I ain't looking for no nigga's pity. I can stand as a man on mine for real."

Phoenix smiled and looked me over. "How old are you?"

"I'm seventeen."

"And how many people you got living in your house?"

"It's me, my sister Jahliya, my auntie Veronica, and my cousin Danyelle. I'm the only male, I gotta hold them down."

"I can respect that more than you know," Phoenix said exhaling. "You graduated high school yet?"

"I got a few more months, then I'll be done."

"What about college? Are you considering stepping your toes into the waters?"

I frowned. "Bruh, why are you asking me all of these questions? I thought I was here so you could put me on?"

Phoenix pulled a stuffed blunt out of his pocket, and lit the tip, cupping his hand to shield the flame from the wind. As soon as it was lit, the scent of the ganja was loud in the air. He took three pulls and inhaled them deeply. "Because I'd rather see you in college than out here in these streets. As long as all of our young men are out in the ghettos hustling, and not attending college, we'll never really see the change that we need. It'll just be this ongoing cycle of dope dealers, and prisoners. All the game is designed to do is keep us in a box where we will forever be slaves to the system. College is the only key our people have to effect change."

"Man, how the hell am I going to afford college if my family can't even afford to keep the lights on in the house? College seems ambitious big homie, I'm just keeping shit real." Truth be told I actually wanted to go to college so I could be a famous movie director and screenwriter. I loved writing, and always felt I would make the best movies that were circled around our people's struggles, and dilemmas.

"Yeah, well, maybe I can help you with the whole college thing and avoid putting you on the streets. If I could do that would you consider taking my help and going hard in them books?" he asked, blowing a cloud of smoke into the air.

"What about today, how do I feed my family tonight? How do I get our stuff back turned on?"

Phoenix dug into his pocket and pulled out a knot of hundreds. He counted out five gees and handed them to me. "Huh, lil' dawg, this yours. Let's just say you owe me one. Right now, I don't know what it's gon' be, and it may not ever be anything, but as of, right now we're good. Take that money and go and get your people right. It's too much shit going on out here in these streets. Shit that you don't need to be part of."

As much as I wanted that money, I didn't feel right accepting anything from anybody without knowing what it was going to cost me down the line. I handed it back to him. "I can't take this shit, bruh, I ain't no charity case. I'm a man! Now I need this money, but I wanna earn it. I ain't accepting no handouts." I held the cash back out to him just as Mikey walked up.

"What the fuck we got going on here?" he asked, looking at the money in my hand.

Phoenix was quiet for a brief second, then sighed. "Aw, ain't nothing, just paying lil' homie a few bucks in advance because he finna be one of the lil' niggas to open up that new trap house in Black Haven. I'ma have Mike-Mike show him how to buss down a brick of the Rebirth, and we gon' get him rolling."

Mikey smiled. "That sound like a plan to me. We need as many of these lil niggas out here working that we can get. The more workers, the more product we can push, and the richer the hood gets. It's the muthafuckin' circle of life." He looked over my shoulder. "Damn, who is that?"

I turned to look and saw Jahliya making her way over to us. When she got to the security barricade, her path was blocked by the men there. I could hear her cursing them out in classic Jahliya fashion. Mikey made his way over there and pushed one of the guards aside.

At the same time, I made it beside him stuffing the money into my pocket. "Yo', that's my sister man."

"That's Jahliya?" Phoenix asked with his eyes bucked.

Mikey held out his hand. "Damn, baby girl, I don't know what brings you out but thank God you came out. You are fine as a muthafucka. Where are you from?" he asked, looking her up and down hungrily.

Phoenix had the same look in his eyes. I could tell they were stunned by how bad Jahliya really was. Once again, I found myself getting jealous, and irritated.

"Damn, she so thick," Phoenix uttered under his breath.

Jahliya popped back on her legs. "That's my lil' brother right there. I was coming over here to make sure he was good. Y'all been over here talking to him for a long ass time."

Mikey smiled. "And she feisty, damn that's hot. I'ma ask you again, where are you from?"

"I'm from, Jackson, Miami and right here in Memphis. What that got to do with anythang?"

Mikey held up his hands. "Say, baby, I don't want no trouble, I was just asking. And for the record your brother good. We gon' put him down with this Duffle Bag shit. All y'all luck is about to change."

Jahliya nodded. "I like the sound of that, but I'll believe it when I see it. You ready to go?" she asked me, ignoring both men.

42

"Say Phoenix, we good here?"

Phoenix nodded. "Yeah, I'ma have you link up with Mike-Mike so he can get you started. Until then you hit them books and get your house in order." He shook up with me and gave me a half hug.

Mikey never took his eyes off Jahliya. "Say Jahliya, what's yo' old man name? I ain't understanding how he could ever let somebody as bad as you out of the house."

"My old man is my brother. I don't fuck with none of these lame-ass niggas around here. Life is too short. Come on JaMichael, let's get out of here."

I walked past Mikey and mugged his ass. I didn't like him already. I especially didn't like the way he looked at my sister. I already had it in my mind that if he ever came at her the wrong way, I would body his ass, I was that heated.

****

That night, I knocked on Veronica's bedroom door around eight o'clock. When I told her, it was me at the door she invited me in. I twisted the knob and stepped into her bedroom holding a candle in my right hand. She sat up and rested her back against the headboard. Her room was full of lit candles, that smelled of Vanilla.

"I'm so embarrassed to have had us in this dark for this long Ghost. I know your parents are looking down on me and shaking their heads." She clutched a big pillow to her chest and hugged up with it.

I took a seat on the edge of the bed. "I been looking for a job auntie. Hopefully one of the places I applied too should be hitting your phone real soon."

"I don't know how they gon' do that because my phone is off. The only way I get any service on it is if I am around Wi-Fi." She shook her head. "Arguing with that damn, Victor, at work was the worst mistake I coulda made— well, second to messing with him, to begin with. I been a certified nursing assistant for two years, now I can't get a job nowhere. It's like those people at the hospital where I worked put the word out. Now don't nobody wanna hire me. I feel so defeated baby."

I scooted up on the bed, placed my arm around her shoulders and allowed her to lay her head on my chest. "I know we going through it, right now, but I promise you things are going to get better. All of this is my fault, I'm the man of the house. I'm supposed to be out there making it happen for our family. Ain't no way we should be sitting in the dark."

"Baby, it's not your fault. You are a child! You're supposed to be focused on school and going off to college. This is my house. I am responsible for paying the bills and seeing to it you have a stable home to reside in. It's just so hard on us women these days. There are so many stumbling blocks placed in our path. If we're lucky not to trip over those blocks, we have to worry about the sea of trifling men that lie in wait. It's exhausting." She nestled up to me closer. "JaMichael, you can't allow yourself to become one of those low life men out there. I know we're going through it, but you are tasked with taking this adversity and using it to become a better man than those you see walking around this ghetto. Do you hear me?"

"Yeah, I do Auntie, I love you. Do you know that?" I asked her kissing the side of her forehead.

She sucked her teeth. "How could you possibly love me? I can't even provide a stable home for you and your sister."

"Don't matter, had you never stepped up we woulda been raised by the state. There was a good chance we would have been separated, and not even know each other. But you took us in, you kept us together, and for that, I will always be in debt to you." I kissed her forehead again and held her firmer.

"I appreciate that, Ghost. One thing I can say about you is that you have always been a very humble child. It doesn't take much before you are expressing your gratitude." She shook her head up under me. "I don't know what the hell I'm going to do about these bills, though. I feel like I'm drowning, right now," her voice started cracking up.

Hearing her sound so weak was beginning to affect me in an emotional way. My auntie Veronica was like my mother. She had been the only mother I'd known since my own mother Blaze had been murdered before I was even a year old. She'd taken us is with open arms, and I loved her just like she was the woman who had given birth to me.

"Auntie, how much money would it take for us to get the lights, and gas back on?"

"Baby don't you worry yourself about that. The only thing you should be focused on is school. Everything else is for me and your sister to figure out," she chastised.

"That's not an answer. How much is it going to take?"

Veronica sat up and eased out of my embrace. She scooted off the bed and stood before me in just her red bra and panties. She placed a hand on her hip. "Boy, what did I say?"

Now I was scooting out of the bed and standing in front of her. "With all due respect, you gon' tell me what all of the bills come to, then as a man, I'ma go out there and make it happen because that's what I'm supposed to do."

She gave me an angry scowl. "Boy, I am grown as hell. I don't need nobody taking care of me. You are my nephew, I said ain't no need for you to worry about how much the bills come to because it ain't your concern. I'll take care of it. Now goodnight, JaMichael." The only time my auntie called me by my first name is when she was heated with me.

It was like she was crazy about calling me Ghost. She'd told me once, it was one of the few things that kept my parents alive to her.

I stepped into her face and placed my forehead against hers as my lips grazed her nose. "Veronica, if you don't tell me how much these bills come to, I'ma show you that I ain't no lil' boy no more."

She jerked her head back in disbelief. "Oh, yeah, and how are you going to do that?"

"I'ma sit my ass on that bed, pull you over my lap and spank that ass until you tell me what I need to know. Now I don't wanna do that, but it seems like you're trying to force my hand. Now I'ma ask you one more time, how much do the bills come to?"

She stared at me for a long time and crossed her arms in front of her chest. "Boy, you gon' do what?"

That was it, I sat on the bed and pulled her by her arm until she fell stomach first across my lap. I adjusted her so that I could trap her ankles and her shoulder blades. Then pulled her panties into her ass and raised my hand as far into the air as I could.

"JaMichael, if you don't let me up I swear to God it's finna be a murder in Orange Mound tonight. You bet not bring that hand down. Boy, let me up!" She jerked against me.

My hand came whirring down until it crashed into her hefty ass cheeks. *Whack!* She jerked and yelped in pain. "I know you didn't just slap me on my ass?"

Before she could go on, I went crazy spanking my aunt with no regard for her hollering or fighting against me. I didn't know where the thought had come from for me to get down on her in such a fashion, but I had to do what I had to in order for her to respect me as a man and allow me to do what I needed to do. By the twentieth slap, she was breathing hard, and biting into my side. She was no longer struggling. She was still, groaning, yet every now and then she would thrust her pelvis into my thigh.

"How much is the rent?"

Slap!

"Uh, it's seven hundred," more heavy breathing.

"How much is the electric bill?"

Slap!

"A thousand, it's a thousand dollars bay—beee!"

"And the gas?"

Slap!

"Eight hundred, unnhhh fuck, Ghost. It's eight hundred!"

I tore that ass up with ten more licks on strength. Veronica was a tough woman. I didn't know how she would get back at me, but I wanted to make things perfectly clear of who was going to be in charge of our house. So, while I spanked that ass, I let her know I was a man, and from then on, she was to treat me as such.

When I finished, I allowed her to get up. She stood before me and turned around. Her brown ass cheeks were hanging out of her panties. They were a bit ashy from my spanking them.

She spaced her cheeks and rubbed them carefully in my face. "Ow, ow, ow, I can't believe you just did that."

I grabbed a bottle of her lotion off her dresser, and squirted a nice amount into my hands, before moving her hands out of the way, and rubbing the lotion onto her backside. "I'm sorry, Veronica, but you be handling me like I'ma lil' kid a something. It's time you respect me as a man. I'm the only one in this household that is."

She turned around to face me. Her breathing was rugged. I reached behind her and continued to rub the lotion into her buttocks. Her gap was right in front of me, I was trying to ignore the fact that I could smell her scent as clear as day. "Ain't no man ever spanked me like that before, Ghost. I wish you would have never done that. You got all types of foul shit running through my brain. I'ma need you to get up out of my room, right now before I make a huge mistake." She took a step back.

The candle lights showcased her hard nipples stretched up against the bra. The material was sheer enough for me to see her entire areolas.

"Gon' now, baby."

I stood up and pulled the five gees out of my pocket. I counted off thirty-five hundred. "Huh, Veronica, this is for the bills, and hopefully there will be just a bit left over for you to have some pocket change. I know you don't want me in these streets, but ain't nothing you can do about it. I gotta make it happen. So, huh."

She stepped back. "I ain't taking that money, Ghost."

I pulled her to me and stuffed the roll of bills into her bra. "Veronica, I understand you're prideful but go and pay them bills. We're in this together, all of us." I kissed her cheek.

She shuddered and fell back taking a seat on the bed. Her hand went between her thighs. "Okay, nephew just go. I'll take care of it."

My last sights were of her getting into the bed and pulling the covers over her body.

Ghost

Chapter 5

I didn't mess with a lot of dudes while growing up. I had a hard time making friends because I honestly felt better being alone if I wasn't with my sister. But when I was in the tenth grade, I became real cool with an out of towner by the name of Getty. Getty was originally from Chicago Illinois and had a habit of calling everybody either Joe or Charlie, even though, that wasn't their name. I guess that was equivalent to how everybody in Memphis referred to one another as Mane, Buddy, Potna, or Homeboy. It didn't bother me because Getty was so cool. In my opinion, he was one of the smoothest niggas that went to our high school. So, it seemed by happenstance that we would link up.

One day as I was coming out of school, Jahliya was outside waiting on me, and it seemed like every nigga that came out had their eyes on my sister. She was rocking this lime green, and grey Polo mini skirt, cheerleading uniform, over a pair of sandals that showed off her pretty toes, and no bra. She made every head turn that came out of the building and had the audacity to be waiting right where the kids loaded on their school buses.

On this particular day, I had just made my way out of the building when a group of dudes from the basketball team sorta surrounded her. They were shooting all kinds of disrespectful comments. Talking about what they would like to do to her, how thick she was, and how they would love to run a train on my sister. I made it there just in time, she was taking her earrings out of her ears, ready to get down and dirty when I rushed into the crowd and pushed the closest nigga in her face up out of it.

"Nigga, if you don't get yo' goofy ass out my sister's face we about to have a major problem," I assured him.

He stumbled back a few feet and caught his balance. He had to stand every bit of six-feet-eight inches tall and weighed no less than two-fifty. His eyes lowered, as he balled his fists. "Nigga, I know you didn't just put your hands on me."

Jahliya finally had her earrings off. She kicked off her sandals. "Fuck you wanna do. You think you finna walk up on my brother like it's sweet? Yeah, the fuck right."

Two teachers rushed over into the crowd of kids that had formed in front of the school. They sent a bunch of threats saying if we didn't clear out they were going to report us to the principal, then had the nerve to pull out their cell phones so they could get our faces on camera. They swore to use them later when they wrote their reports. So, like chastised kids, we filed out. As me and Jahliya were walking away the tall basketball player told me to meet him at Washington Park so we could knuckle up without being interrupted. Before I could respond Jahliya told him we would beat him and his crew there, and sure enough, we did.

We waited for five minutes before cars began rolling into the parking lot. High school kids jumped out of them expecting to see a show. I ain't gon' even lie, I was nervous as hell because this nigga stood six-feet-eight inches tall, and I was sure he was good with his hands because he was so big. On top of that, I'd watch my sister get into a few females asses, and she was a beast in every sense of the word. I'd only had a few fights, and they weren't all that. So yeah, I was nervous as a puny kid fighting a schoolyard bully.

The crowd followed us until we were standing in the middle of the basketball courts. This big nigga took his shirt off, and he looked like he had muscles on top of muscles. He had to be doing some type of steroids. His body was impossible looking.

He cracked his knuckles and rolled his head around on his neck. "Let's get it, fuck nigga. Arrgghhh!" He roared like a Lion.

Jahliya backed me up and stood in front of me. "Fuck that big ass nigga, JaMichael. David and Goliath!"

"What?" I was confused looking over her shoulder as he bounced up and down on his toes and began shadowboxing. Now I was really nervous. Before this, I'd only heard of shadow puppets.

"David and Goliath, remember the story in the Bible where the small boy slayed the big giant after the giant underestimated him. That's the same thing that's going on here. Don't believe in his strength, believe in Jehovah's, and you gon' kick his ass. And if you don't, I'm jumping in and they gon' have to whoop both of our asses."

"Hell, n'all, you chill, I got this nigga. But even if he whoop me, let me handle my bidness like a man. I can accept an ass-whooping. He just gon' have to whoop me every day. That's on my mother."

Jahliya took my face into her soft hands. "You got him, lil bro. I love you, now whoop that nigga for me." She kissed my cheek.

I pulled my shirt over my head and balled my fist as tight as I could. I stepped into the circle just as Tamia came inside of the fence. She forced her way through the crowd.

"No, no, no, JaMichael, you ain't finna fight, Bam big ass. Hell n'all, let's get up out of here." She took a hold of my wrist and began to pull me away just a tad, but I made it difficult.

Jahliya rushed over and pulled her off me. "Let my brother go. Fuck how big that punk, Bam is, he ain't spooking nothing over here. JaMichael, whoop that nigga."

Tamia tried once again to get a hold of me, but Jahliya wasn't going for it. She yanked her back aggressively, and that was that. "Now go, JaMichael."

I threw up my guards and shielded my chin. Before I could even think about my first move Bam swung, and his fist went through my guards and caught me on the jaw so hard I stumbled backward with my face ringing like a telephone. That shit hurt so bad I wanted to pick up a weapon.

"Yeah, bitch ass nigga, shit just got real didn't it," he cracked. The crowd cheered his name, as he came toward me in a boxer's stance.

"Get that nigga, JaMichael, here he comes!"

Come he did, that fool rushed me full speed ahead swinging haymakers. He was swinging so hard, I coulda sworn I could hear the sounds of his fists cutting through the air. He caught me twice in the left rib, and once in the right, before rocking me in the left jaw, knocking me to my knee. I could taste the blood in my mouth.

"Aw n'all, you punk ass nigga. You done knocked my brother down. Fight me, you finna have to fight me!" Jahliya yelled, rushing to my side.

Bam laughed like a giant. "Man, this bitch hilarious. Somebody come get this ho before I knock her ass out too. The homie don't discriminate." He started laughing again.

"JaMichael, are you okay? Please say you are," Jahliya whimpered.

"Look at that bitch crying over that soft ass nigga. She got a fat ole' ass. Look how the wind blowing her skirt up, damn I'm fucking. Watch!" This fool had the nerve to slap Jahliya on her ass and squeeze her booty.

54

She jumped up and got ready to go at him, before she could I was up, pulling her back. Now I was heated. My jaw hurt, my ribs hurt, and my pride felt even worse. "Come on, nigga, let's get it."

He mugged me and threw his guards up. I knew he was getting ready to rush me like he had been doing, but I promised to be ready for him this time. His guys from the basketball team cheered him on, told him to smash me, and they promised they'd sexually wreck Jahliya next after they finished me off. Bam waited until he'd gotten ten feet away from me, lowered his head and rushed me like a raging bull swinging blow after blow.

I waited until he was in striking distance and dropped to the ground, with all of my might I swung and punched him right in the nuts, then leaned in, and kicked his left knee in. He buckled and hollered out so loud birds flew from the trees. I jumped up, took a hold of the sides of his face and kneed him as hard as I could. Blood spurted from his nose, as he fell back.

The whole crowd was silent as a library. They stood in obvious disbelief. Bam sat on the ground with his knee facing inward, and his hand between his thighs clutching his jewels.

"Fuck that, finish him, JaMichael. Finish his bitch ass for slapping me on my ass," Jahliya was hyped with revenge on her mind. Her eyes were glossy and devilish.

Before I could follow her commands, two of Bam's guys rushed me and started fuckin' me up. Every time I hit one of them, the other one hit me, and this went on until I ran out of breath. Then Jahliya jumped on one of their backs and bit a plug out of his cheek. She locked on like a Pit Bull. Two girls from the cheerleading team jumped on her, fuckin' her up, as two more from the basketball team jumped on me. I had somehow managed to get up, swinging. They were rocking me, but I was fuckin' them up, too. Finally, it became too much, and they dropped me and proceeded to stomp me out when Getty came out of seemingly nowhere on bidness with a nightstick in his hand. He cracked one with the stick, and punch another. Within seconds we were fighting all the dudes side by side, dropping they ass. When he got tired, he dropped the stick, pulled out his Glock, letting loose in the air.

Bocka! Bocka! Bocka! Bocka!

The crowd took off running in every direction. I fell on my ass bleeding from the face, out of breath. I crawled over to Jahliya who laid on the ground laughing like she was going mad or something.

"Them bitches fucked me up. They got me, JaMichael, I ain't even know they got down like that." She started laughing some more before she stood all the way up.

Me and Getty got real cool after this, I asked him why he opted to help me? He said he ain't like Bam, or none of his niggas because they were bullies, and fuck niggas. In addition to that Bam had fucked with Getty's sister Aliza back in the day. She told Getty, Bam tried to force himself on her one night after a party while Getty was in the detention center for an armed robbery he'd caught as a juvenile. Ever since then Getty said he'd been looking for a way to get at Bam's head, and this was only the beginning.

****

When Mike-Mike pulled in front of Veronica's crib blowing his horn on a muggy, and rainy Sunday night, Getty was just about to knock on the door. I peeped through the window and met up the homie on the porch. We shook up, he eyed Mike-Mike's car and looked back at me. "Who Dat nigga here to see, Joe?"

"Me, I'm finna start getting money out in Black Haven," I said grabbing a cheap Poncho from the coat rack in the hallway.

"When you start fuckin' wit' them Duffle Bag niggas?"

Mike-Mike blew the horn again. "Most recently, a mafucka had to do something. We ain't got none of our shit on in here. I gotta make a way for these women and myself. You know how the game go." I hugged him and stepped back.

"Nigga, my household ain't doing too good either. What I gotta do to be down with them? I'm tired of hitting licks."

I shrugged my shoulders. "I don't know, but I'll find out, let me holler at, Mike-Mike real quick." I went down the stairs and shook up with Mike-Mike through the passenger's window. "What it do, fool?"

"You Mane, let's get da fuck up out of here. You got rain popping all on my leather seats and shit," he snapped.

"A'ight, damn, that's my bad. But check this out, my homeboy trying to be down, too. What do you say you put him on just like you finna put me on?"

Mike-Mike maneuvered his head until he could see past me. "Mane, I know that ain't that stickup nigga, Getty?" He pulled his Cartier glasses from his eyes and squinted. "Hell, yeah, it is. We don't fuck with stickup kids in the Duffle Bag Cartel. Stick up kids bring way too much drama and baggage along with them. The Cartel is strictly about life hustlers and go-getters. Tell that nigga he ain't invited to the promised land and hurry up. Time is money."

I felt incredibly disrespected. I turned around and jogged up the steps to the crib. "That fool, tripping. He saying they don't fuck with stickup kids."

Getty sucked his teeth. "It's all good, fuck them, niggas, then. I'll get at you whenever then." He started to walk off. Getty was a big, gorilla-sized nigga, with dark skin, and grey eyes that made him look spooky.

"Wait a minute," I said stopping him.

He turned back around. "What's good?"

"Dawg listen, whatever they hit me with you already know, I'ma hit you with enough to get right. You're my brother and I got your back homie. Know that."

Getty's eyes lit up. "Stand on that shit, bruh. A mafucka starving just as bad as you are, right now. If you eating then yo dawg should be eating, too, straight up." He hugged me and spun off.

I watched him disappear around the block before I jogged back into the rain and jumped into Mike-Mike's whip.

"I'm letting you know, right now, JaMichael if you're fucking with us, you gon' have to cut dude bum ass loose. It is impossible to war and make money at the same time. You have to be dedicated to one or the other, and the Cartel is dedicated to money. Let's roll, you got a lot to learn, and a short time to do so."

Chapter 6

The lights and gas had been back on in the house for a full two weeks, it felt like heaven to be able to walk around with everything functioning properly. I knew I had a lot to learn about becoming a man, but I felt like every day that passed, I was getting closer and closer to discovering what my purpose was for me, and the women in my house. Ever since the spanking episode had taken place between me and Veronica it seemed like things were a bit weird. She acted differently around me for some reason.

The second week, I was hustling for Phoenix, he paid me twenty-five hundred dollars. I took fifteen hundred and caught Veronica just as she was beginning dinner one night, while Jahliya was in the bathroom finally getting a chance to enjoy a hot shower. I slipped behind her, grabbed her and kissed her on the neck playfully.

She shuddered in my arms and slapped them just a tad. "Boy, don't be sneaking up on me like that. You know that Orange Mound getting crazier and crazier by the day."

I wasn't trying to hear nothing she was talking about. "Man, you're my auntie. If I wanna sneak up on you and snatch you up like this every day, that's just what I'ma do. Besides, I ain't gon' never let nobody hurt you. I love you way too much for that." I kissed her again and held her for a moment, while the chicken continued to fry in the skillet. Then I slipped from behind her and counted out fifteen-hundred-dollar bills. "Huh, this for you."

"What, baby? Unh-unh, I can't take this. You just paid all of the bills for the month. Now you giving me more money. Ghost, hell n'all, please hold onto your money baby."

"A'ight now, you must want me to spank this juicy ass again?" I said grabbing her by her globes, pulling her close to me.

Once again, she began breathing hard. Her eyes were closed. She slowly opened them and looked into mine. "Okay, nephew, just give me the money before you start something that's gon' get us in trouble. I mean you do know, this is the south, right?" she asked rhetorically.

"Yeah, and?"

She leaned forward and rested her lips on my ear like Mrs. Jamie had. "Well, baby your auntie was raised in the south, and every time you touch or grab my ass the way you're doing you make me feel things, I know, I'm not supposed to be feeling. So, I'ma ask you again not too, baby. I'm trying very hard to control myself." Her hot breath felt good on my ear.

It gave me tingles all over my body. I didn't know why I was playing around with Veronica the way that I was. I knew it wasn't right, but I think deep down inside of myself I had always been attracted to her in that forbidden way. She was so sexy, to say the least, and she had a habit of always wearing next to nothing around the house. Her body was so righteous, I could never get enough of looking at her. I felt like something was seriously wrong with me.

I moved my ear away from her lips and slipped my hands under her short nightgown, kneaded her cheeks like dough, before slipping them into her hot crease from the back. Her lips rubbed against my fingers, as I pressed forward so she could feel how hard I was. I didn't know if I would go beyond those boundaries and actually fuck her but playing around was definitely heating me up.

I placed my lips on her ear now. "Veronica you raised me. Now, look how I'm feeling all over you. You know you been ready for me to do this to yo' sexy ass body ain't you. You want this young meat, I feel how wet your pussy is." I licked around her ear canal and slid my tongue as far inside of it as it would go.

She dug her nails into my sides, and humped backward on my fingers, making the middle one go inside of her an inch or two. "Ghost, you're driving me crazy, baby. I can't take this." She slid her hand down and grabbed my piece through my shorts, then yanked her hand back as if she'd been burned by fire.

I heard a noise behind us and looked to see Danyelle stepping out of the hallway. I didn't even know she was there this week. Me and Veronica broke apart, as she came into the kitchen with a slight smirk on her face.

"Mama how close are you to being done? I'm freaking starving out of my mind?"

I slipped past them and into me and Jahliya's bedroom. My piece was so hard, I pulled it out and stroked it a few times. Blowing air out of my jaws because I was so frustrated. As I was putting it up, Jahliya came into the room.

She caught sight of my front and blushed. "Damn, lil' bro, what got you all hot and bothered?"

She opened our closet door and stood before it in a towel. Even her ass was looking right all poked out of the towel the way it was. It wasn't helping my boner go down at all.

I was super frustrated. "I gotta hit up, Tamia. She finna give me some pussy tonight or I'm finna go crazy."

Jahliya had been smiling at my frustrations, but after I said this part, she stopped and frowned. "Here we go with you sweating this bitch again. You don't need her." She locked our bedroom door by placing a butter knife in the door jamb. Then she dropped her towel. She took her hand

and ran it over her bald cat. It looked juicy and plump. "I just shaved her in the shower. What do you think?"

Now my dick was jumping like *Kris Kross*. I grabbed it and held it to my stomach. "Damn, Jahliya, why you fuckin' wit' me, right now? Can't you see I'm struggling?"

"Can't you see that you don't have to be? Damn, I wish they wasn't here, right now, but come here," she ordered.

I slowly walked over to her until I was standing in her face. Once there she grabbed me by the waist and brought us face to face.

"Do you love me?"

"Hell, yeah I do! You already know that" I groaned in torture.

"I don't need to hear all of that, just answer my question. Do you love me?" She looked into my eyes and unbuttoned my shorts.

"Yeah, sis, I love you more than anything in this world."

She pulled me all the way out and squeezed me in her little hand. "Damn, it's so hot and so big. I can't believe this is attached to you." She slowly stroked it up and down, licking her juicy lips, then she shocked the hell out of me when she lowered to her knees.

She kept stroking my meat, then stopped. "I love you, too, JaMichael! You don't need no other bitch but me. You can want them hoes, but you don't need them. The only woman you're supposed to need is me, just like the only man I will ever need is you. This world don't get us. They never will look who our parents were." She brought the head of my pipe to her lips and kissed it. "Mmm, this that forbidden shit, right here." She kissed it again and licked all around the head, before sucking me into her mouth.

My knees got so weak I buckled and nearly fell on my face. She kept a stronghold on my tool. "Boy, sit on the bed, and let me show you a thing or two. Remember, I'm only doing this because I will do anything for you. Matter of fact lay back."

I followed her commands and laid back on the bed. She crawled beside me, grabbed ahold of my manhood again and wrapped her ankle around my right ankle. Her hot breast rested on my waist. I could feel its hard nipple, then she was sucking me nice and slow, pumping my piece at the same time.

I closed my eyes and started moaning deep within my throat, it felt so good. Her little hand pumped me up and down. The fact of who she was kept on adding to my arousal. It felt so good. "I love you, Jahliya! Unnhhh—I swear—to God—I love you—"

She sped up her movements and rubbed all over my stomach, then both of her hands were resting on my abs while she slurped me like a pro, in a matter of ten minutes I was cumming. All the noises and the scent of her sent me over the edge. She pumped me faster and swallowed my seed. When she took her mouth away, she continued to pump me until a tiny drop of semen appeared at the top of my head, then she licked it off, and swallowed that too.

"Damn, you drive me so crazy lil' bro. I don't know what the fuck has gotten into me." She looked up to me. "Are you okay?"

I was still shivering in disbelief. Had Jahliya just did what she did, or was I tripping? Either way, I needed more of her. We had already gone this far. I wanted to sacrifice myself for her just like she had for me.

"Jahliya, I wanna taste you, sis."

"Boy, what?"

I sat up and rubbed on her thick thigh. "I wanna taste you. So, gon' head, lean back, and let me do my thing." I slid my hand between her thick legs and rubbed her box. It was leaking at this point. Her lips were heavily engorged.

"Wait, JaMichael, I don't know about that. I mean I shouldn't have done what I just did, but it is what it is. But I'm good."

I came to my knees, picked her lil' ass up and tossed her back on the bed. She bounced twice, then scooted until her head was resting on the headboard. She opened her thighs as wide as she could and planted her feet on the comforter.

I snuck my head between them and kissed her bald pussy smushing the lips. She moaned softly. I didn't know the first thing about eating pussy. I wanted to make sure I was giving her as much pleasure as she gave me.

So, as I swiped my tongue up and down her slit, I swallowed her savory juices and stuck my head up. "Jahliya, I don't know how to do it, teach me."

"What JaMichael?" Her face was flushed. She squeezed her perfect titties together and pulled on the hard nipples.

"I'm serious, I want you to teach me how to eat pussy so I can please you whenever you need me to. Your kitty so fat, and I just wanna make sure I'm doing it right." I kissed her box again. "Damn, it's so fat, sis."

"Mmm, I know, and I'm dying for you to eat me, Ja-Michael. That big ass dick got me fiending. Okay, just listen." She spread her lips and exposed her glossy bubble gum pink to me. "You see this lil' nipple at the top of my slit?"

"Yeah." It stood up like the tip of a pinky finger.

"Well, that's my clitoris. All of your focus and attention needs to be on it at all times. I like it licked in circles, and sucked medium, not too hard, and definitely not too soft, you have to split the difference, but start out by licking it really fast."

I took a whiff of her pussy's scent and got harder. Then I leaned forward and flicked my tongue over her clitoris as fast as I could. "Like that?"

She bucked into my face. "Yes-yes-shit—yes," she hissed.

I rolled my tongue around her button over and over again. Sucked it medium like, and felt her juices dripping off my chin. She grabbed a pillow from the bed, and placed it over her mouth, screaming into it. I grabbed her thighs and proceeded to make oral love to Jahliya's pussy, while she rode my face from her back. Her scent kept getting stronger and stronger. It was driving me crazy. She came twice real hard and threw the pillow off the side of the bed.

Then she pushed me back and straddled me. My dick stuck up in the air. "I can't give you none of this pussy lil' bruh. We'd be doing too much, but I can let you feel my heat." She opened her lips and trapped my dick head inside of them, as soon as it was there she laid on my chest and ground her pelvis into mine juicing me. It felt so good.

"Mmm-mmm, baby bruh! Mmm—you feel that heat? Huh, shit—I wanna—fuck you—so bad!" She humped into me faster and faster.

My dick slipped into her hole, she stopped, and pulled it back out, it was leaking with her secretions. I prayed for her to put it back in. But she didn't, she kept going until she came all over me.

I flipped her over and rubbed myself all over her wet box while I stroked him. She held her lips open for my sight. The more I looked between her legs the harder and more excited I became until I came all over her cat, and stomach. She rubbed it into her skin and pulled me down so we could French kiss each other. We collapsed to the bed, breathing heavy.

Jahliya got up a short time later and opened a window and turned the fan on so that it blew our forbidden session outside. Then she lit two incenses, climbed back in the bed with me and cuddled up. "I love you, JaMichael. I wish we could go all the way then I wouldn't ever have to fuck with nobody outside of you. But that'll be doing way too much, don't you think'?"

I was feeling so good I didn't care what the world said. I'd never in my life seen a female harder than Jahliya, and the fact that I was able to lay in the bed with her and do all of this forbidden shit was enough to make my head explode. "To be honest sis fuck the world. I love you, and one of these days you gon' give me some of this, right here." I rubbed her kitty again and sucked my fingers into my mouth.

She moaned, "Damn, you so nasty."

There was a knock at the door. "Y'all wake up in there. My mama said the food is done, it's time to eat," Danyelle said, before stepping away from the door.

Jahliya pulled me to her again. "Don't worry, bruh, sooner or later we gon' cross that bridge anyway. It's in our DNA, you already know we can only avoid the inevitable for so long." She kissed my lips. "I don't give a damn about this world. All I care about is you. We're all we have."

"That's how I feel too, sis. Always have, and I always will." I held her in my arms for about five more minutes, then Danyelle beat on the door again, so we broke apart, and went to dinner.

Chapter 7

After hustling for a month, I got in the habit of keeping no less than five hundred dollars in my pockets at all times. For me, that was a dramatic change because prior to Phoenix and his Duffle Bag Cartel crew, I ain't have shit in my pockets but lint. So, it felt real good to not be broke, although it was hell holding onto the money because it always seemed as if things were coming up out of the blue. Since it was hard for Veronica to find work, me and Jahliya had to basically keep up with the household bills in order to keep things afloat. It didn't really bother me as much as it did Jahliya. I felt Veronica had been taking care of us for years well before either of us was able to work.

So, I took it upon myself to stick fifties, and hundred-dollar bills in Veronica's purse whenever I could. I'd also went as far as two months ahead on each bill to give us a bit of breathing room. Jahliya spent most of her money on groceries and necessities for the house. After handling all of those things she was basically broke, so I found myself sneaking money into her purses, and pants pocket as well. It didn't bother me I was finally starting to feel like a man because I was providing for the women of my household. That meant the world to me.

Getty rolled up on me one Tuesday afternoon as I was on my way into the house. He tapped his horn and rolled down the window to his busted up Chevy Blazer that his pops had left him before he got locked up. I was just getting home from school and wanted to knock out my homework as fast as I could, so I could hit up the trap house over in Black Haven. I had two gees stashed, and I needed at least two more if I was going to cop me a decent whip within the next few weeks or so.

When I came down to the truck, I could feel the heat coming out of it. "What it do, fool?"

Getty shook his head. "Say, Joe, I need you to roll with me for a minute so we can talk."

"No, can do bruh, I gotta get my ass in the crib so I can finish up this homework. This is our last assignment before finals next week." The homework along with the classic project I'd completed with Tamia was going to be twenty percent of my grade. There was no way that I could risk fucking it off.

"JaMichael, I ain't trying to hear none of that shit, bruh. I'm going through some shit, and I need to holla at you. It's important." He looked desperate.

I'd never seen my homie look that stressed before. "A'ight, let me run this shit in the house, and I'll be right back out to fuck wit' you." I took my bookbag off my shoulder and rushed up the steps.

When I got into the house the first thing, I smelled was cologne. I found that odd because the only person that wore cologne in our house was me. Then I heard Jahliya laughing, followed by the sound of a deep ass voice. I got heated right away. I made my way into the living room and was met with the sights of Jahliya sitting on the couch in a mini skirt that showed off most of her thighs. Her legs were crossed, and I could even see were her caramel skin began to turn a darker shade of brown on the underside of her thighs. Sitting across from her was Mikey, Phoenix's right-hand man.

When she saw me, she jumped up and came to me. "Hey, lil' bro? How was your day?"

I looked past her into Mikey's eyes. He picked up a bottle of Moët and sipped out of it. He had an icy, gold Rolex on his left wrist and a bracelet with yellow diamonds on his right one. His neck was cluttered with three gold ropes, the charm piece was a duffle bag with money coming out of the bag, it was sprayed in green and clear diamonds.

"What's good lil' homie? You on yo' way to the Trap in a minute?"

I ignored him and pulled Jahliya out of the room, and into the front room. Outside Getty blew his horn I guessed to rush me along. I ignored him, too. When me and Jahliya were in Danyelle's room, out of earshot, I went off on her ass. "Sis, what the fuck dude bitch ass doing in here with you? And why the fuck you got on this lil' bitty ass skirt for this nigga?"

Jahliya's eyes got bucked, then she frowned. "Ja-Michael, who the fuck you think you talking too like that? Don't forget I'm your big sister. I'm grown, and I ain't gotta answer to nobody. Not even auntie since I'm paying all of her fuckin' bills."

"We are paying all of her fuckin' bills. You ain't doing nothing on your own. And that ain't answering my question. Why the fuck is he here, and why you got on this lil' ass skirt?" I pulled at the material until she slapped my hand away.

She sighed, and lowered her head, then looked up at me without saying nothin' for a short while. "Look, these niggas always trying to get at me. They always talking about how fine I look and offering me the world. It's time I cash in on some of that shit. Why shouldn't I?"

"Because you don't need none of them fuck niggas for shit. That's why I'm out here busting my ass every single day." I felt myself getting heated. Not only was I feeling inadequate, I felt like my sister was choosing another nigga over me. That hurt my heart.

"JaMichael, that's how the game go. I don't love none of these niggas. Secondly, you shouldn't be the only one hitting my pockets. You're my lil' brother, I should be hitting yours, not the other way around."

"I don't care about that shit. Look, I see how that nigga be looking at you. He on some smash and dash type shit. I ain't going, tell dude bitch ass to leave our crib. I got you, I don't need no help."

She shook her head. "Nope, I can't do that. Well, I could, but I'm working on something, right now. You know how I am, I gotta have top of the line everything, whether we broke or not. I need him to fit the bill, and until he does I'ma kick it with him for a minute."

"So, you finna let him play you and smash yo' lil' ass all for some clothes. Man, I'll knock yo' ass out. Don't play wit' me." Now I was really getting heated because Jahliya was sounding stupid. She sounded like the average ghetto bimbo. I wasn't having that shit, I didn't give a fuck if she was older than me or not.

She laughed. "Ghost, I know you're all angry and shit, and maybe even a bit jealous, but if you put yo' hands-on me you already know we gon' tear this house up. Secondly, boy dudes don't run the game, it's us women that do. Everything a man does is for a woman, or because of a woman, even the gay men. Hell, they love us so much they wanna be like us. But listen, Mikey is a joke, he's egotistical, self-centered, and easily breakable. He got so many insecurities that he's easily penetrated, I got him. You need to have faith in me, not in men. I'ma hit his pockets for a few weeks, and that's gon' be that."

"That's gon' be that, huh? So, he ain't gon' get the pussy?" I really wanted to know the answer to this question because I felt real possessive of Jahliya, especially since we'd tiptoed on that forbidden line. That had excited me, and I wanted more. I was seeing her through new eyes. I was needing her more than I wanted to admit.

"I ain't say all that. Who knows, only time a tell." She smiled.

I mugged her for a minute, then shook my head. "Man, fuck you. Do what you do, I'm finna do me."

Before she could hug me, I brushed past her. I wasn't trying to hear shit she was talking about no more.

"JaMichael—JaMichael! You better bring yo' ass back here. JaMichael!" Were the last words I heard before I left the house feeling like a sucka.

I jumped into Getty's car, steaming. "Let's roll nigga, damn."

"Fuck wrong with you?" he asked starting the ignition, looking over to me.

"Nothing just drive, I don't feel like talking about that shit." Not that I could with him anyway.

Everything I was feeling had to remain locked inside of me. The thing about that was, I didn't even know what I was feeling.

"Dawg yo' sister just came out of the crib. I think she looking for you," Getty said, lowering his head so he could see up on our porch.

"Drive man," I demanded.

"But she coming down the stairs."

"Drive nigga! Fuck is you deaf?"

Getty stormed away from the curb leaving Jahliya standing in the exhaust. "Look bruh, I know you feeling some type of way and all of that, but you gon' give me my respect. I ain't finna be dealing with yo' funky attitude all day."

"Anyway, what's good? What you wanted to holla at me about?" I said this dryly.

In the rearview mirror, I could see Jahliya standing in the middle of the street in front of our house, then she slowly walked away with her head down. That made me feel sick. I was thinking maybe I had gone too hard on her.

"I'm fucked up, JaMichael. I need to get my hands on some serious paper."

"Serious paper like what?" I wanted to know.

"Eight to nine thousand. My shorties need clothes, shoes, and a bunch of other shit. The bills are way past due. We been in the dark for three days now. I still owe eight gees in birthing expenses alone, and my PO sweating me about those fees. Something gotta give."

I didn't have nowhere near the amount he needed. "So, what do you have in mind?" I rolled his passenger's window all the way down, so I could get some cool air on my face. I was so stressed out over Jahliya, I needed to cool down.

"Well, I got a few things on my brain. I'll run each by you. First, I was thinking you put me on the hunt of one of those niggas in the Cartel. Help me hit they ass for at least ten bands, that oughta hold me over for a lil' while."

I looked at him like he was crazy. "What else you got?"

"A'ight, since you're opposed to that you could come out to Nashville with me. We can hit this lick that my cousin Parker got lined up for me." He sniffed and pulled on his nose.

"What's this lick pertaining to?" I really didn't feel like getting involved with Getty's crazy ass.

He was always doing something out of the ordinary, and his enemy count had to be through the roof. I kept hearing Mike-Mike in the back of my mind when he said it was impossible for a person to make money, and war at the same time.

"We could come up on a few pounds of some Loud. I'm talking like ten. Zips are going for three hundred in the hood. So, off that ten pounds, we're looking at forty-eight thousand dollars. That's twenty-four bands apiece pending everything goes right."

"Twenty-four gees? Are you sure about this?" That sounded like real good money to me.

I hadn't even seen twenty gees as of yet. So, to imagine me having twenty-four was something to think about. I could give Jahliya twelve of the twenty-four, then she wouldn't have to depend on Mikey to do nothing for her. First, I wanted to make sure this move was authentic because Getty had a habit of putting a hunnit on ten. He stretched the truth a lot.

"Hell, yeah, I'm sure man. Parker works for his connect, right now. All he do, is maintain the safe house for them. He knows how much work they got in there at all times because he is in charge of the exporting and sending out mass orders daily. Unlike you, Parker is willing to let me lay his ass down, in exchange I'll owe him a favor."

"A favor. What type of deal is that? Do you even know what the favor will be?"

"Nope, I never do, but it'll probably be me having to clap a nigga for him a something. He always beefing with them hillbillies down there. Who knows? So, are you in or out?" He pulled into the lakefront and cut his ignition.

He pulled a thin cigarillo from his shirt pocket and sparked it. It smelled like mostly paper. It started to hurt my head right away. The homie was definitely hurting. He took four quick pulls and passed it to me.

I took it and flicked it out the window. He hollered and got ready to go out and get it until I pulled a fat ass Dutch from my pocket and sparked it. I'd stuffed a whole quarter into the one blunt, well, actually Phoenix had, but it was mine just the same. One pull and I was lifted.

I took another one and gave it to him. "Huh, that's you," I said with smoke rising from my mouth. I didn't like putting my lips on something another nigga had put his lips on. That always made me feel weird, so I didn't do it.

He grabbed it with a smile on his face. "Still are you in or out?"

"Long as you make sure everything is cool I'm in, but if I make anything less than twenty-four thousand I'ma be real irritated. So, you better have your ducks in a row. But I'm most definitely with you."

"That's all I need to hear. We roll out tomorrow night, so be ready."

Chapter 8

That night when I got home Jahliya was waiting up sitting on the living room couch, reading a book called '*A Bronx Tale*'. As soon as I stepped into the house, she stood up and walked over to me.

I was about to walk around her when she sidestepped and got into my path. "JaMichael, we need to talk about what happened earlier."

I was ready to dismiss her ass because I was still feeling a little jealous. All I saw every time I blinked my eyes was images of her sitting across from Mikey with her skirt around her plump thighs. I had to get out of the house.

"We ain't got nothin' to talk about. Shouldn't you be somewhere kissing that nigga ass, so he can buy you an outfit a something?" I shook my head and stepped around her.

She took hold of my arm and pulled me back to her. "Look, JaMichael, I don't know what the fuck is going on with you, but you ain't gon' be talking to me like I'm one of those thots out there in the street. Now, I know you're feeling some type of way but you're still going to give me my respect that is rendered to me. Do you got that?" She asked pointing her pinky finger at me.

I refused to look into her eyes, I was irritated. I wanted to say a few more things that would piss her off, but I decided against it. I didn't like hurting Jahliya's feelings.

She was still my heart no matter how disappointed I was with her. "Anyway, what we need to talk about?"

She took hold of my hand and led me to the couch. We sat side by side. She took a deep breath and exhaled slowly. "Look, JaMichael, I really don't know what to say, but you already know how I am. You know I gotta have top of the line everything. I don't like you fitting the bill for every-thing. I feel like I'm gold-digging my own brother."

"Jahliya, it ain't about all that, though. You're my sister, I don't love nobody in this world more than I love you. You're the reason I'm out here chasing all this money. I'm supposed to make sure you're good. That's my job as a man. Fuck I look like having you going out, playing house wit' a nigga just to get a few outfits? That shit weak."

She stood up and ran her fingers through her hair. "Damn, JaMichael, you forget I'm the same way though. I don't like to depend on nobody for nothing either. I wanna take care of you just as much as you take care of me. After all, we are in this together. So, if I can hit these nigga's pockets why wouldn't I?"

I got up and looked down at her. "Man, where auntie at?"

"Her and Danyelle went out to eat. They won't be back until later tonight. Why do you ask?" She rested her hand on my shoulder.

"I just wanted to know where she was, it ain't no big deal. Anyway, if you wanna go and fuck with Mikey on some gold-digging shit, go right ahead. I ain't gon' stop you. You do you, I'm finna do me." I grabbed my phone out of my pocket and started to text Tamia.

I asked her if she wanted to get together and study, then I sent her a bunch of emojis letting her know what I really had on my mind, as I stepped into our bedroom so I could get dressed.

Jahliya came in behind me and slammed the door. "Ja-Michael, what the fuck is wrong with you?"

I ignored her and started getting ready. I was thinking, I would throw on a nice Polo outfit, that way they could

76

match my boxers. I hadn't done much, but I was still thinking I would jump into the shower.

She came and stood in front of me once again. "Ja-Michael, do you hear me talking to you?" Now she was grabbing my shirt into her lil' hand.

I yanked it off me. "Don't touch me like that, shorty." I bumped her lil' ass out of the way.

"Damn, you really are acting all stupid because of this shit with, Mikey. I ain't never seen you act so pussy in my all your life. Nigga, you need to get it together, and holla at me like a man. Or we about to tear this mafucka up."

I laughed under my breath. Jahliya was a beast when it came to getting down with her hands, but she ain't have no win with me. I knew she had to know that. "Sis, I ain't fuckin' wit' you, right now." My phone buzzed right in front of her.

I picked it up and looked at the screen. Tamia had sent a text saying her mother was out until noon tomorrow. That Tammy, her mother was working two jobs back to back. A big ass smile spread across my face. I was trying to hear nothin' tonight, I had plans on getting that ass.

Jahliya tried to grab the phone. "Who the fuck is it that got you smiling like a dummy, right now?" she snapped.

I turned my back to her and texted Tamia to come and pick me up asap. "Don't even worry about it. This grown folks bidness." I laughed, pulled my shirt over my head, then pulled my pants off, and grabbed my drying towel.

I was thinking I might as well jump in the shower, so I could be fresh and clean after all. I walked past Jahliya, and ran the shower water, closed the bathroom door, set my phone on the back of the toilet, and got ready to jump inside when she came in butt naked.

"Fuck is you doing, Jahliya?"

"Nigga, if you ain't finna talk to me out there then you can talk to me in here. I ain't got no problem with it, and I honestly don't care if you do either." She pulled the curtain back and stepped inside the shower. The water beaded off her caramel skin. "What is you waiting on? Come on and get yo' ass in."

I stood there for a second, then relented. I got inside the shower behind her. She backed all the way up until her booty smushed against my piece. She manipulated it from side to side. I felt myself getting hard and had to back up.

"So, tell me who you was over there texting? Was it, Tamia?" She had me backed into the shower wall now her ass moved up and down in a slow rhythm.

I closed my eyes for a second. My piece was getting harder and harder to the point it was throbbing against her. I pushed her forward a bit. My pole stuck straight up. "Jahliya, stop playin' wit' me. Get yo' ass out of this shower, so I can handle my bidness, and get up out of here. Tamia, a be here in a minute."

She smacked her lips. "You already know I don't give a fuck about that. Far as I'm concerned, she can wait on you all night. Ugh, you always running to her lil' prudish ass every time something ain't going right in this house like she's your saving grace or something. She ain't on nothing. She ain't finna do shit but have you walking around here with blue balls, watch."

I grabbed the body wash and squirted a nice amount into my towel, before placing it under the hot water, then I was lathering my entire body. "Jahliya, I ain't finna go there with you. It is what it is. I need to get out of this house for a minute."

She stepped into my face with the water popping off her shoulders. She took hold of my piece and started stroking it. "I'm saying, JaMichael. What do I gotta do to keep you in the house tonight? You already know I ain't trying to let you go off fuckin' wit' that bitch. Not on my watch. So, what is it gon' take?" She kissed my neck and continued to stroke me, but now she was adding a lil' thumb around my head. That move kept on sending tingles all through me. I had to hold on to the shower wall while she did her thing. She took some of the lather from my body, and applied it to my piece, stroking it faster and faster. Her teeth bit into my neck. "Tell me, JaMichael!" Just tell me, bruh!"

I allowed her to work me for two minutes, then I pulled her hand off my dick. "Stop, stop, stop, gon' man."

She looked at me dumbfounded. Her hair had curled up from the water. "What you saying, JaMichael? You saying it ain't nothing I can do to keep you in this house tonight?"

"N'all, I'm saying get yo' lil' ass out of this shower, so I can finish doing what I gotta do." I pointed. "Gon', you already said we won't be crossing that line anyway."

The water continued to rain down on Jahliya's hair. She took two hands and wiped her face clean. "You know what, fuck you den, JaMichael. You wanna treat me like I don't mean shit to you, it's all good. Gon' head and fuck wit' that bitch for the night. I think I'll take Mikey up on his offer and hit up Club Platinum. You know since everything is on him." She stepped out of the shower and grabbed the towel, I'd brought into the bathroom for me. I watched her ass jiggle before she wrapped it around her supple body. She made her way out of the bathroom.

"It's all good. Just make sure you make that nigga pay for everything. That's the way the game is supposed to go anyway," I retorted, stepping under the showerhead.

"From now on, I ain't gon' worry about what you're doing, and you don't worry about what I'm doing. That's how we gon' do this. From here on out we're just siblings." She closed the door behind her.

I remained under the water with a whole bunch of things going through my mind. Apart of me wanted to go out there and check her lil' ass. I wanted to prevent her from going out with Mikey, but my pride wouldn't allow me to. So, instead, I showered and got fresh. By the time Tamia pulled to the curb to pick me up, Mikey was rolling up to the house in a Porsche truck to snatch up Jahliya.

****

Tamia stood in front of me, sucking on her bottom lip. She wore a pair of purple, lace boy shorts that were all in her gap. "What's the matter with you, JaMichael? I thought you'd be happy to finally be spending a night with me?" She straddled my lap, so we were face to face. Then took her hands and placed them on the rounds of her ass cheeks.

I inhaled the scent of her perfume and shook my head. Jahliya had my mind all kinds of fucked-up. Every second that passed, I was wondering how far Mikey had gotten with my sister. Deep down in my heart, I was sure all he wanted to do was fuck, that didn't sit right with me.

"Baby, you must not feel like talking. If that's the case then where does that leave us?" she asked kissing my cheek.

"I don't know, I just got some shit that's captivating my mental, right now. But you know what, let's do our thing." I kissed her lips, sucked all over her neck, picked her up and straddled her.

80

She moaned, "Open my bra, Daddy. Go ahead and pull my titties out, I love when you suck on my nipples."

She ain't have to tell me twice. I popped that bra, pushed her titties together and sucked on her hard buds one after the other while she groaned within her throat.

"Unnhhh, Daddy, damn that feels so good. I think I'm ready, feel me down here." She took my hand, scooted back and pushed it between her thick thighs until I was rubbing her pussy through the panties. It felt hot and pudgy.

"Hell yeah, Boo, that feels real good. You think you ready for daddy, huh?" I sucked her neck.

"Yes, I'm ready." She opened her legs wide and humped upward.

I kissed her crotch, and sniffed hard, before licking the material. In my mind, and in that moment, I was trying to do anything to take my mind off Jahliya. Thoughts of her had me captivated. I hated myself for feeling the way I was feeling. If I found out Mikey had so much as a hand on her, I knew I was going to lose my mind. Now my fingers were pressing the material further into her sex lips. Each one appeared the crotch band was stuck between her gap as if it was a thong.

"Go ahead, Daddy, taste me. If you do me, I'll do you."

While those words would have sounded good to any dude in my position, it didn't sound so good to me cause Tamia wasn't all that cold when it came to going down. Now that Jahliya had shown me how to eat a cat the right way, I felt like I woulda been doing Tamia a service that she couldn't duplicate for me. I was already feeling stubborn because of Jahliya.

"N'all, ma, how 'bout you do me first?"

She groaned in frustration and pulled down her lace panties. "Baby, come on, I need you. I promise if you get me right, I'll let you do whatever you wanna do to me tonight. That's my word." She opened her thighs wide and continued to stroke her kitten. I watched a finger slip into her about halfway, she pulled it out and sucked it into her mouth. "Deal?"

Man, her monkey was looking so good I found myself game for anything. I crawled closer to her and rested my cheek on her thigh. From this position, I could smell her scent loud and clear. Some manipulating of her folds, and she started to purr like a kitten. "Unnhhh, baby, please just do anything to me. I need you!" She held her own lips open and flashed her pink.

I moved closer and located the small nipple at the top of her valley. Then I kissed it and ran my tongue in circles around it. Tamia was already moaning loud and humping into my face. She had her thighs over my shoulders going nuts. It made it hard for me to breathe.

"Unnhhh, unnhhh, it feels so good! It feels so good—unnhhhh—unhhhh!" She started to quake and shiver.

I slipped two digits halfway inside of her. This really seemed to push her over the edge. Her screaming became so loud I wanted to tell her ass to shut up.

When I finished, she sat up and pulled me on top of her. "I'm ready, I don't care no more. Come on, JaMichael. Please!"

She didn't have to ask me twice, in a matter of seconds I found myself all the way nice and ready for action. She was oozing, and ready to go, and so was I. I leaned in, sucking on her neck, at the same time I placed the head at her opening, and tried to push.

She tensed up and pushed my chest. "Ssszzz, wait Ja-Michael, I don't know about this anymore."

"Come on, Boo, just let me get the head in, and it's gon be smooth sailing after that." I tried to inch in some more. "Ssszzz, wait, I think we need too—" She pushed hard against me again.

I jerked my hips forward, and about three inches went inside of her. She felt hot and sticky. Her nails dug into my sides. "See, baby, we're almost there." She was tight as vice grips.

She tried to pull away from me. "No, I'm not ready, Ja-Michael. It hurt too much, I thought I was, but I ain't." She pushed me as hard as she could and twisted from under me.

My piece popped into the air, I was so frustrated I felt like hollering and punching the wall. Instead, I got up and grabbed my clothes while she pleaded for us to try again. I ignored her and bounced without saying a single word. Tomorrow was a new day.

Ghost

Chapter 9

"Joe, let me say in advance I appreciate you coming all the way down here wit' me. I know you don't need to be doing this shit. But it's good to know, if I need you, you're going to have my back. This means the world to me dawg," Getty said pulling the Chevy Astro van to the curb and throwing it into park. He reached over so we could shakeup.

"It's good, bruh, long as the money is going to be exactly what you said it is. I can definitely use those twelve gees. I got a lot of shit on my plate, right now." I looked out the side window and surveyed the dark street.

There was only one streetlight in the middle of the block. It musta been faulty because it flashed on and off. The street was narrow and lined up with one level mobile homes. We were all the way in Nashville Tennessee. I felt real uncomfortable because I didn't know nothing about this city. I didn't know what to expect from the move that we were about to put down, but I wanted that twelve bands, and I was willing to do anything to get it.

Getty looked at the clock on his dashboard and looked over his shoulder. "Man, where the fuck is, Parker? He shoulda been here already," he continued to rubberneck as he looked over his shoulder.

I scanned the area some more and saw a figure appear from the side of one of the mobile homes. As soon as it did, I upped the forty and placed my finger over the trigger. I wasn't even sure, I knew how to use it, but if anything popped off out of the ordinary, I was sure I would find out on the spot.

"Say, bruh, it seem like somebody creeping from the side of that mobile home right there."

Getty cocked his Glock and aimed it toward the back window. "Hell yeah, I see what you see. Mafuckas must think it's sweet." Getty was a natural killer.

He'd told me that he'd killed his first nigga when he was only eleven years old. He never went into too much detail, but from what I gathered, he'd smoked his sister's boyfriend a day after her boyfriend had beat her into a coma. He also said, for him killing was easy. He said every time he smoked somebody it made him feel like he was killing his sister's boyfriend all over again.

Getty snuck low to the floor of the van, and opened the side door, before jumping out, and rushing toward the figure. He made it to the figure in what seemed like record time, grabbed the person by their clothes and pushed them into the darkness. I could only see them a little bit after Getty stuck his pistol to the figure's head. I remained inside of the van feeling my anxiety go through the roof. Whatever took place, I was hoping he didn't have to kill this person. I looked both ways and prayed the police didn't roll-up. By the time I looked into the direction where they had been, Getty had released the figure and both men were making their way back to the van talking cordially.

When they got inside, Getty tucked his gun back into his waistband. "Say, JaMichael, this is Parker right here. Parker, this is JaMichael. He's going to be the one handling this bidness wit' me."

Parker extended his hand, and I shook it. "JaMichael, you ain't got nothing to worry about this is going to be short and sweet. I am going to go into my normal post, and you guys are going to come in there about thirty minutes later and lay me down. The door has two locks, both are about halfway up the door. Instead of me locking both, I'll only secure one. All you'll have to do, Getty, is kick that bitch as hard as you can. It's going to come inward. I'll be the first person you see on the other side of the door. Lay me down, along with the two young teenagers that are going to be in there. If anything looks suspicious, I'll let you know with a look like this." He bucked his eyes and blinked them nearly five times in a row. "There ain't no guns in there yet, so y'all ain't got nothin' to worry about."

Getty nodded. "Man, this shit is a piece of cake. This ain't my first rodeo. Nor will it be my last. We gon' be in and out of there in a matter of minutes, you can bet yo ass on that."

I ain't gon even lie, I was sitting there nervous as hell. I had never done anything like what we were about to do. I didn't know what to expect, what to think. I was wondering about my own toughness, like if something happened would I really be able to buss my gun and take somebody out? When in all actuality I had never even shot the thing before. My brain was all over the place, yet, I was trying my best to remain calm.

"That's really the gist of it. Get in and get out, and everything will be cool. Deal?" He shook up with Getty and gave him half of a hug, before patting him on the back and sliding out of the van. Before he closed the side door he said, "Oh, and it was nice to meet you, JaMichael. Hopefully, we'll see each other again soon under better terms?" Then he closed the door and jogged back off into the darkness.

Getty ran his tongue across his teeth and nodded his head up and down. "Yeah, it's gon' be sweet. JaMichael, you ready to handle this bidness?"

I nodded. "Mane before we do though, I need to know what we gotta give Parker out of this deal?"

Getty waved me off. "I already told you, I'll owe him a favor somewhere down the line. That's for me to worry about, not you. You just get your mind right before we go in here and lay this Loud spot down. A'ight, Joe?"

"Yeah, a'ight Getty," I retorted, looking out of the passenger window surveying the strip once again.

****

Getty had me a little nervous when he turned on the ignition and drove five blocks before pulling into an alley and cutting the ignition. The alley was cluttered with old couches, and a mattress that I assumed had been pissed on by a little kid of some sort. I grew nervous because I thought we were going to buss the move in the spot where there was nothing but mobile homes. But this new area we were in looked grimy, and low down. Before he pulled into the alley, I saw that there was more than a few of the houses boarded up. Their gang was spray-painted on the stop sign, and the alley was full of people's discards. The alley even smelled pissy as hell.

Getty cocked his gun again and looked over at me. "We in and out, my nigga. It's as simple as that. Come on, stay close behind me. You see anything unusual, you smoke that shit. I mean don't hesitate, use the whole clip if you have to. Matter fact—" He dug into his pocket and handed me another magazine clip. "Huh, this way if you run out of the first one, you'll have a whole other ass clip to run through."

I took it and slid it into my spring jacket pocket. Getty pulled a mask over his face, and seconds later I was doing the same. We jumped out and ran down the dark alley. He was a few feet in front of me. We jumped over the mattresses that smelled like strong piss and continued to run. Two cats saw us coming and ran in different directions. They scared the shit out of me. I aimed the Glock, and almost shot one of them. My heart was beating fast as hell. Getty continued to jog when he got into the back of the Trap house, he hopped the metal gate, and rushed to the backdoor of the house, trying to catch his breath. I got beside him a few paces later.

He pulled his gun from his belt and slid along the side of the house. When he came to the front, he climbed onto the porch. I followed suit, the first thing I noticed about the front of it was that there was a money green Jaguar SUV parked, with twenty-eight-inch gold rims that were still spinning as if the person had stepped out of it only a few moments prior.

Getty looked both ways and took a step back. He held the side of the door jamb for leverage, then kicked it in as hard as he could. The door popped inward just a tad, but it was still hanging on by the lock. Getty raised his foot again, this time he kicked it with all of his might it seemed, because as soon as the door flew inward, he hollered out in pain, and fell to his knees. "Aawww shit!"

I rushed past him, and into the house with my Glock aimed in front of me. "Everybody get the fuck down! We come for the bud, but don't mind taking lives, play wit' it!"

Parker was inside with three other people. There were two dark-skinned dudes that looked as if they were eighteen. Both were heavy set with dreadlocks. They threw their hands in the air and backed against the wall. The third dude was high yellow, with green eyes, and curly hair. He stood there unmoving, mugging me, and when Getty stood beside me he mugged him too.

"Say, Mane, y'all best bet is to get the fuck up out of here before you lose your lives. Dis ain't what you want right here, Potna. I'm telling you that, right now." He brushed off his Versace suit and adjusted his gold belt. In his right hand was a bottle of Moët.

When I glanced over at Parker he was giving me the bucked eyed look, and signal that he told us he would give if he felt anything was happening out of the usual.

Getty brushed me out of the way and aimed his gum at the light-skinned dude. "Say, Joe, you heard my mans. He said get yo' punk ass on the ground along with everybody else. And if I was you I'd watch them statements homie. Say something like that again, and I'm smoking you."

The high yellow dude curled his upper lip. "Nigga if you rob my spot where the fuck is you gon' go? I run this whole state. It ain't no muthafucka in Tennessee that don't know who *Screw* is."

Getty smacked him with his pistol and pushed him against the wall. He cocked the hammer of his weapon. "I don't know who the fuck you are, and I don't care. We come for this bag, and we'll take yo' life to get it." Getty snatched him up and placed his barrel to his temple. "Now lay yo' punk ass down, and don't get back up until we're finished here." He slung him to the floor with so much aggression, that he landed awkwardly.

There was blood already coming out of his mouth. It slid down his neck, and I could see that he was missing a tooth. "This some bullshit."

"Nigga, just stay yo' ass down, and shut the fuck up," I ordered, placing my foot on the back of his neck.

Getty snatched up Parker and flung him into the kitchen. "Watch these fuck niggas in here, Joe. If anybody move, don't hesitate to stank they ass. That's an order!" He rushed into the kitchen where Parker was just starting to get up. "Tell me where the Loud at! Don't play wit' me, I swear to God, I'll put two in yo' head, and keep it moving."

From a distance, I could hear Parker complying with his demands. I took a step back, with my gun aimed on the trio in front of me. I was praying that Getty hurried up. I had a bad feeling in my stomach, and nothing felt right about the whole set up. I started sweating and could feel my heart beating faster and faster.

"Nigga, hurry yo ass up, damn!"

Parker was eased back into the living room five minutes later. He had his hands in the air and a worried look on his face. "That's everything man. You cleaned out the whole safe. Now get the fuck out of here!"

One of the goons from the floor, looked up and frowned at Parker before speaking, "Nigga you gave this pussy nigga my father's merch? Really? You don't know it, but you just wrote your own death warrant. You might as well get as far out of town as you possibly can because it's over for you homeboy. Believe that." Screw couldn't believe Parker's ass was so weak.

Getty threw Parker to the floor and stepped to his left until he was standing over Screw. "Get yo' ass up, tough guy."

Screw looked up at him and looked off. "You ain't talking to me, homie. You already a dead man walking, and that nigga is, too. As a matter fact, all y'all are dead, that's what that is right, thurr."

"Oh, you really think so? You really think it's a wrap for us?" Getty asked.

"Just get out of here. Please, we don't want anymore, trouble," Parker said giving Getty the signal look.

Getty waved him off. "Man, fuck that, dude thinks he tough as hell. I don't know where you from, or what you be about homie, but one thing for damn sure, I'll never let a man walk away from me after he done promised to take my life. You can tell yo' daddy to kiss my ass." Getty aimed at Screw's face and fired three quick shots that knocked Screw backward. His head jerked twice, then blood was pooling down his neck before he slumped on his side appearing to be lifeless.

I stood there frozen, my eyes were bucked wide open. I couldn't believe Getty had killed a man right in front of me.

Parker jumped up and rushed over to Screw. He checked the pulse of his neck. Felt all around it and looked back at Getty. "Getty, what the fuck did you do? Are you crazy? Do you know who that is?"

Getty grabbed the black garbage bag that was filled with the Ganja and threw it over his shoulders. "Hell, n'all I don't, and once again, I don't care either. Life goes on. Come on, Joe, let's whack they ass, too." He stepped to his left and stood over the two dark-skinned dudes that were laying on their stomachs with their hands above their heads.

Before he could harm them, they both jumped and took off running before jumping through the front windows of the Trap house. Getty rushed behind them firing away.

His gun jumped in his hands as shells popped into the air. "Come on, JaMichael buss, bruh. What the fuck is you waiting on?" He jumped through the empty window and was off into hot pursuit of the two fugitives.

Parker went back to checking Screw's neck for a pulse. "I can't believe this shit man. I can't believe this. I knew I shouldn't have fucked with, Getty's, crazy ass." He shook his head, stood up and punched the wall hard. The drywall caved in around his knuckles.

I didn't know whether to stay there to see what was going to take place with Parker or to follow Getty to make sure he was okay. Before I could make a decision, I heard four loud pops. Seconds later Getty came through the front door that was already caved in.

"Come on, JaMichael, let's get the fuck out of here."

"You fucked me over, Getty! I can't believe how you fucked me over!" Parker yelled as we made our way out of the Trap, and to the whip that was waiting for us.

As we were running down the street, I saw the body of one of the dark-skinned dudes. He was twisted on the pavement with blood leaking from the wounds in the back of his head.

Getty stopped and looked down on him. "That other nigga got away. That's okay, though. I'll be back in Nashville for the next month until I find his ass. I ain't never been one to leave one behind."

Looking down on the dead dude's body had me both spooked, and fascinated. I had never seen a newly dead body before. I had been to funerals, but I had never seen a body that was still warm to the touch and leaking.

Chapter 10

That night, after I got back home to Memphis, I couldn't sleep for shit. Not only was the botched lick fresh on my mind, but when I got home, Jahliya wasn't there as of yet. That pissed me off more than I could explain. I was heated, and on top of that, I was worried about her like crazy. I laid there in bed until about three in the morning. I kept replaying the sight of how the dark-skinned dude looked on the concrete. I felt like the image would be burned into my brain for the rest of my life. I don't know how it happened, but somehow, someway I wound up falling asleep. I was just starting to doze really good when I felt a hand on my bare chest. I became cautious and sat up in the bed breathing hard. Sweat peppered along the side of my forehead.

"Lil' bruh, what the hell is wrong with you?" Jahliya asked, sitting beside me. She smelled like perfume and marijuana.

It took a second for me to gain my consciousness. When things started to make sense to me, I stood up and closed the door to our room. "Where the fuck you been?" I asked with a little more fire than I intended to render down on her.

She exhaled. "Aw shit, here we go with this. Look, Ja-Michael, I don't feel like doing this shit with you. I'm tired, my feet hurt, and life is too short." She rolled her eyes, pulled her new Burberry dress over her head and dropped it on to the floor. Underneath she wore nothing but a thong. Her big nipples were erect on her breasts. She walked to her bed and pulled back the covers.

I slipped out of the room, and down the short hallway that led to Veronica's room. When I got outside of her door, I placed my ear to it. I could hear the sounds of Keith

Sweat, and her fan going. I figured she was sleep, and that was all I needed to know. When I got back to my bedroom, Jahliya was sliding under the covers, yawning. I grabbed them and pulled them off her body.

"I don't give a fuck what you thought you was finna do, but one thing is for damn sure, and that's that, you're about to tell me what the fuck you did with tonight, Mikey," I demanded after closing our room door.

Jahliya sat up in the bed and scooted all the way back until she was resting up against the headboard. "Really, Ja-Michael, we really finna do this?" She asked obviously irritated.

I didn't give a fuck. I was super jealous, and angry as hell. "On some real shit, all I wanna know is if you let that nigga fuck?" I asked.

"What?" She sounded caught off guard.

"You heard me, sis. Did you let that nigga smash you? It's a simple yes or no?"

Jahliya laid on her side and tried to pull the cover back over her. "Boy, you tripping, you need to take your ass to sleep, clearly you're deprived."

I slapped her on the ass hard and yanked the covers away, slamming them to the floor. "Stop fuckin' playin' wit' me, Jahliya! Did you let the homie smash or not?"

She slid out of the bed and balled up her little fists. "Ja-Michael, I'm sleepy. I don't feel like arguing or doing this with you tonight. I'm about to get some sleep. We can do this in the morning. Goodnight." She turned to walk away from me.

"I watched a nigga get his head knocked off today, sis. It fucked me up. Every time I close my eyes all I can see is his face, and the face of the other that was left on the pavement. I'm sick, I needed you to be here when I got home, but instead, you was out fuckin', Mikey."

She stopped in her tracks and turned around. "Ja-Michael, where the hell was you that all of this shit took place?" Now she was standing in front of me. She circled her arms around my waist and rested her head on my chest. "Were you in any danger?"

I sighed and hugged her. "Sis, did you fuck that nigga?"

She led me over to the bed and sat beside me. "Ja-Michael, I'm just gon' keep shit real with you—" She paused for a little while, then exhaled loudly. "I like him, JaMichael. I know what his reputation is in the streets, but I really think I can change all of that. I'm already hitting his pockets. Look what he gave me." She jumped out of the bed, picked up her Birken bag, rifled through it, and came out of it with a bundle of cash. "Huh, count this."

I was so sick, all I could do was push her hand away from me. I didn't like when other males did for Jahliya. I felt like I was the only man she was supposed to lean on, and now that Mikey was in the picture, I felt emasculated. "So, I guess the answer to you fuckin' him is yes?"

She shook her head. "N'all, we ain't got that far just yet, but it could be possible in the near future. Who knows? That's not important, right now. What's important is what you were saying to me earlier. What happened to you tonight? Where did you see all of this stuff take place?"

I was so sick, I didn't even want to talk about it. "Man, I'ma fuck wit' you in the morning. I don't feel like talking about it, right now. It's good that you and that nigga, Mikey, hitting it off so well. One false move toward you and I'ma kill his ass. That's my word," with that said, I ignored Jahliya for the rest of the night, and went to sleep on her ass while she tried to ask me a million questions in different ways of why I was mad at her?

I didn't utter another sound. Finally, she gave up and stormed back to her bed talking a bunch of shit under her breath.

****

Getty woke me up early the next morning with his face all sweaty and shit. He'd been beating on the door like he'd lost his mind before I opened it. As soon as I did, he walked right past me, and into the living room.

"Man, JaMichael, I think Parker bitch ass told Screw people what went down. I been getting some real weird phone calls all last night, and this morning. Mafuckas talking about what they gon' do to me when they catch me and all of that shit. And I know they had to get my information through him because he's the only nigga down in Nashville that got my shit. Damn, I think I fucked up. I shoulda whacked his pussy ass along with the other two. Now I gotta worry about this whole situation. We might have to take another trip there to clean up this mess."

I was thinking, Getty had to be out of his mind. I had to be at school in less than forty-five minutes, and even if I didn't, I wasn't trying to get involved with his goofy ass.

"Bruh, if dude do anything he ain't supposed to do that shit falls on you. That's *your* mans. You made it seem like Parker was *so* one hunnit. Now you running around here worrying about if he finna rat you out to them mafucka we hit. Dawg!" I slammed my fist into my hand. "You need to get yo' shit together."

Getty couldn't do nothing but shake his head in understanding. "I know, bruh, but apparently Screw was the son

98

of this major nigga from out West named J.T. Supposedly he's a big Tymer out that way. I don't even know the nigga, but whoever he is, he got Parker all freaked out. I think I might gotta change his ass over."

Whenever a nigga from Chicago used the term Changing Something Over, that meant to murder that person. To send them into the next life by any means. "Well, bruh, you gotta do what you gotta do. What's good with that Loud, though. When we finna pop that shit?" I wanted to know what was good wit' my bread. That other shit he was talking, I felt didn't have nothin' to do wit' me seeing as it was between him and Parker.

Getty had a book bag on his shoulder the whole time. He handed it to me. "Huh, its four pounds in there of that topnotch Miami Heat. That shit going for three-fifty a zip. You can do whatever you wanna do wit' it. I'm selling my shit in dimes. This area in need of some good Loud, and I'm finna be that nigga. But you do you." He extended his hand, and we shook up.

I let him out the door and finished getting myself together. By the time Tamia was knocking on the door, I was just opening it and sliding onto the porch.

She saw me and walked right up to me, kissing my lips. "Hey, daddy! How did you sleep?"

She smelled so fuckin' good. "I slept good, baby. How about yourself?" I asked cuffing that big ass booty.

She moaned into my neck. "I slept good as well."

As we were walking down the steps of the porch, Mikey pulled up to the house in a fire red Jaguar, with the top dropped. The sunlight shined directly off his dark face. It already felt like it was a hundred degrees out. He was banging Money Bagg, and his trunk was knocking so loud

I could feel the vibration in the concrete. I sighed as he hopped out of his whip and came around to me.

"What's good, Shorty, say is yo sister ready to go yet?"

I clenched my teeth. "Nigga, don't call me Shorty. I use that terminology when I address females," I said ready to crush this rich nigga.

He held up his hands to shoulder level. "Damn, my bad Mane, a mafucka ain't mean nothin' by it. I won't call you that shit no more. You ain't gotta worry about that." The sun's rays caused the diamonds around his neck to twinkle in the light. It looked like rainbows coming off his jewelry.

Jahliya came out of the house rocking a tight ass Fendi dress that clung to every curve. I don't know what she'd put in her hair, but she had it looking nice and curly. It looked as if it were full of sheen.

She came down the stairs, and wrapped her arms around Mikey's neck, then she was kissing his lips for what seemed like a year, while he rubbed her ass so much that he caused her skirt to rise. Both of her ample ass cheeks revealed themselves to any onlooker that wanted to see her charms.

"Damn, nigga, can you not have my muthafuckin' sister's skirt all raised up like that?" I snapped stepping over to them and pulling the material down.

Jahliya broke her kiss and wiped her lips. "Damn, that's my bad lil' brother. But shouldn't you be headed off to school?"

"Yeah, baby we're going to be late. Let's get out of here." Mikey chimed in.

****

I couldn't think about nothing in class other than Mikey and Jahliya. I hated that nigga for fuckin' wit' my sister. I knew I was on some sucka shit, and I didn't even care. School for me that day was a breeze because I couldn't focus. When it came time for all of the students to leave, Mrs. Jamie asked me if I could stay back so she could talk to me?

I waited until the entire class had departed before I walked up to her desk. "What's good, Mrs. Jamie?"

She looked past my shoulder and stepped out of the classroom. "Let's keep it moving guys, school is over." She stood in the hallways directing the traffic out of the building, then she stepped back into her classroom and closed the door. She came and took a seat at her desk, crossing her thick thighs in her skirt. "What's the matter with you, Ja-Michael?"

I frowned at her. "What are you talking about?"

"Baby, I could tell you were very distracted today. Is it because of our little thing we did?" She asked poking her bottom lip out.

I shook my head. "Absolutely not, I just got some things going on at home that's messing with me, right now, that's all."

"You care to talk about it?" She kicked off her red pumps and began rubbing her toes through her stockings.

I didn't know what it was about older women, and their toes being encased in stockings, but the sight of it started to drive me crazy. I felt my shit getting hard as a brick. "N'all, Mrs. Jamie, I wouldn't be able to explain it to you even if I could. I just gotta clear my head, I'll be alright." I glanced back down at her pretty toes and felt my manhood jump like it was trying to come out of my pants.

She looked me up and down and licked her lips. "Mmm, okay then. I was just hoping you weren't feeling some type of way about what happened between us, but since it's not that. I guess I gotta let you go on about your day. I mean after you rub my feet for me." She smiled at me.

I looked into her eyes and felt kind of shy. It felt like she was always catching me doing something. "What?"

"Boy, you're so transparent. You don't think I see how you're looking at my lil' feet? Well, I do, and I wanna let you touch them. Huh." She held her right foot out to me. The way she had her foot in the air caused her skirt to fall backward, exposing most of her thigh. The sight began to drive me absolutely insane.

I looked over my shoulder toward the classroom door. "You fa real? What if somebody come and catch me rubbing them?" I asked feeling giddy.

She shook her head. "Don't worry about all of that. Besides I made sure the hallways were clear. You better hurry up, baby."

"Say no more." I stepped up to her and before I could take a hold of her foot, she rubbed it against my front, right over the lump in my pants. It felt so good, I didn't wanna touch her foot from fear of it stopping her from making me feel so damn good.

She licked her lips and smiled. "You like that shit don't you, baby?"

I nodded. "Hell, yeah, you know I do."

She brought up both feet. This made her skirt go all the way back so much so, I could see her red lace panties. She was now using both feet as she began to manipulate my front. "Go ahead and pull it out. I wanna see what you working wit'. I know you be driving, Ms. Williams crazy.

I see how head over heels in love with you she is." Williams was Tamia's last name.

I took another look at her classroom door and noticed that the blinds were pulled most of the way down. If somebody wanted to look inside of her classroom, they would have to literally bend down to peer inside. I threw caution to the wind, stood in front of her, and pulled my manhood out. Then stroked him in my hand, hoping I measured up to her standards because after all, she was a grown-ass woman.

She moaned deep within her throat. "Boy, you don't understand how much discipline it takes for a teacher to sit here in front of you fine ass young men, all wet and shit, and not be able to touch you when I want too. It drives me literally insane, especially you, JaMichael." While she was saying this, she ran her toes all over my penis head. Then she ran it up and down the underside it. "How does that feel, baby?"

I had my eyes lowered into slits. "It feels good, Mrs. Jamie. It feels so fuckin' good." She took both feet and used them to work my dick up and down. It felt so good, I was trembling.

She scooted forward on her chair, and grabbed my pole, stroking it. She leaned forward and kissed the head. "I need to spend some alone time with this lil' young meat right here. Boy, I'll show you some thangs to really drive them lil' girls crazy." After she said this, she licked all around it and sucked me into her mouth enveloping me with her intense heat.

I shivered and reached out to hold on to her desk. That's when she really began bobbing her head up and down in my lap giving me the best head of my young life. She was sucking me all wet and loud, while her fingers played inside of her panties.

I was groaning like crazy with my eyes closed. When I felt her tongue tickle my pee hole, I could no longer take it. I started to cum hard, holding onto her desk. My eyes shot open, and when I looked ahead, I saw the face of Bubbie. She smiled, as she crouched down to peer through Mrs. Jamie's door. When our eyes locked, she shook her head and stepped away from the glass.

Mrs. Jamie swallowed everything I pumped out of me. She squeezed my piece in her fist and pulled it upward until a drop of semen appeared. She licked off the final remnants and smiled.

She moaned and exhaled loudly. "Yeah, I'ma have fun with yo' lil' fine ass." Her fingers worked in and out of her box rapidly. She pulled down her panties so I could see her work herself over while she rested my dick against her cheek. Minutes later she came with a short, loud scream.

Chapter 11

When I got outside Tamia was waiting and looking angry. I walked up to her and kissed her on the lips. "What the fuck is wrong with you?" I asked, placing my arm around her lower waist. There was a light breeze, even though it was hot as hell outside.

We began to walk down the block. "About twenty minutes ago that bitch, Bubbie, came out here with a big ass smile on her face. When I asked that bitch what she was grinning at, she gon' say that she was grinning at a completed fool. I don't know what that meant, but it made me feel some type of way. You know I hate her," Tamia said, balling her little hands into fists.

Tamia and Bubbie had gotten into two fights last summer while they were away at cheer camp. They were both bad, and damn near looked alike. Rumor had it they were fighting because they were in fierce competition with each other to see who was going to be cheerleading captain, and who was going to be placed at the top of the pyramid? I didn't know how true that was, but ever since they'd gotten back they'd been beefing. It didn't help matters that Bubbie had been my girlfriend once in the eighth grade.

"It's all good, baby, you ain't gotta worry about her. You already got the biggest prize you could ever ask for." I kissed her on the cheek. "Oh yeah, how do you figure that—and where is this big prize?"

"You're walking with him. I can't see nobody but you, Boo. You're all that matters."

"Aw, do you mean that, baby?" She asked looking up at me.

I nodded. "One hunnit percent, ain't nobody got shit on, my baby."

She stopped so we could kiss. While we were doing so Bubbie pulled up and stopped her brand new, hot pink Range Rover, that was sitting on twenty-eight-inch Faccios. She lowered her mirror tints and turned down the *Cardi B* track that was banging out of her speakers. "Say JaMichael, what it do lil' daddy? Why don't you come mess with me for a minute?"

Tamia tried to break out of my grasp. "That's it, daddy. I'm finna kill this punk bitch!" She did everything she could to break free of my grasp again.

"Whoa now sweetheart, it ain't that type of party. I ain't come down here to start no bullshit with you. I just need to holla at JaMichael real fast. Then y'all can go back to doing what y'all do."

Tamia wasn't trying to hear that. "Bitch, what the fuck you need to talk to my man for? Go and get yo' own nigga, straight up."

Bubbie looked past Tamia. "Anyway, can I holla at you for a second, JaMichael? It's important."

"N'all, Bubbie, my girl ain't feeling that shit. I'll have to get at you another time," I said, wrapping my arm back around Tamia's waist.

Tamia smiled at me. "Yeah, let's get the fuck out of here, baby. This bitch ain't even worth my time." We started walking again.

Bubbie started to roll slowly down the street. "JaMichael, it's about what just happened after school. You know, with Mrs. Jamie's class and all of that." She peered devilishly into my eyes and smiled.

What she said caused me to stop in my tracks. "What do you say, JaMichael? Just for a few seconds."

I knew she had me by the balls. I looked down at Tamia, and into her pretty eyes. She'd worn a little mascara to make her almond eyes pop. She looked so fuckin' fine, with her hair blowing in the wind like it was. "Baby, let me fuck with her for a minute."

"What?"

"Yeah, I just wanna see what she talking about," I said already knowing we were going to argue about this later.

Tamia slid away from me and looked into my eyes angrily for what seemed like five minutes. Then she smacked her lips. "You know what, JaMichael, I don't give a fuck what you do. I guess I'll see you later." She waved me off and kept it moving.

I didn't feel like getting into a big debate with her. I would have plenty of time for that shit later. I wanted to see what Bubbie was on.

I walked to Bubbie's Range Rover, and she popped the passenger's door open for me. The first thing I noticed when I got inside was the fact that her red thighs were juicier than I remembered. As soon as I closed the door, she pulled away from the curb pounding *Cardi B.*

I sat back and allowed her to drive for a minute before I turned her music down. "Say shorty, what's good with you? Why you fuckin' wit' my girl and shit?" I asked, wanting to know what she was up to.

"We'll get into all of that later. What I wanna know is how did things start with you and Mrs. Jamie?"

"I don't know what you're talking about," I lied, looking out of the passenger window.

She sucked her teeth. "Boy, don't play wit' me. I watched our teacher suck the skin off your big thang. All I wanna know is how did that shit get started between y'all? And how can I be down with you, JaMichael?"

I looked her over from the corner of my eyes. Bubbie was light-skinned, with hazel eyes. She had natural, long hair that fell just below her shoulders. For as long as I'd known her she always kept her hair and nails done. She was also a dresser. I loved females who could put an outfit together. I was into dressing myself especially now that my funds were starting to get better.

"Man, why you all up in my bidness? You already got my girl all mad at me and shit."

She shrugged her shoulders. "And? Answer my questions."

"Firstly, it don't matter how shit started wit' me and, Mrs. Jamie. Secondly, you already know I'm fucking wit', Tamia, the long way. Why you tryna get at me all of a sudden?"

She sucked her teeth. "Boy, Tamia ain't on shit. As far as I can see she ain't put you up on nothing. Y'all still walking to school every morning, and she still the only one without a whip. If you was fuckin' wit' me I would change all of that. You too fine to be walking." She rested her hand on my knee. "So, I'ma ask you again, how can I be down?"

All types of shit started running through my head. I knew that Bubbie's father, Timmy had been recently indicted. It was rumored that before the Feds got him, he'd buried a shit load of cash somewhere in Memphis along with a bunch of guns and dope, but I didn't know how true that legend was. Bubbie stay fitted, and well put together. I couldn't really see any major downfalls to messing with her other than the fact that she and Tamia didn't get along. On top of everything else, she was fine.

"Seem like it's taking you a long time to make up your mind? I'll tell you what. Why don't you roll to my house after school tomorrow? We'll get familiar with each other and I'll run some things by you that should pique your interest. Just give me a few minutes of your time, if you don't like what I'm putting down, you ain't never gotta say another word to me ever again. How does that sound? I mean regards to business only of course? I gotta see what this thang like right here no matter what. Even if I gotta pay for it. You feel me, daddy?" Her hand traveled from my knee, all the way to my piece, where she pushed it against my thigh and began stroking it through the pants.

She had on this cute lil' Von Dutch top that made her golden titties look real good and plump. Before any logic came to my brain, I was agreeing, I would be there.

****

When I made it to Tamia's house, she was pacing back and forth inside of the living room with a funky attitude. I could tell she was mad because she was talking under her breath and clutching her lil fists off and on. I tried to be cute, and step into her path, but she wasn't on that shit.

"JaMichael, get the fuck out of my way. I can't believe you had the nerve to leave with that bitch, knowing me and her don't get along. Damn you!" She continued to pace.

I really didn't feel like arguing with her. Tamia had this thing where when she got mad about something, she could dwell on the same thing for days and days. Even after I thought we had gotten an understanding about them. The worst thing I could do was tell her she was dwelling too long. That would really get me in trouble, so I was already preparing for us to be going at it for a while over her feelings toward me having any type of involvement with Bubbie.

"Baby, look I'm sorry. Shorty trying to put me up on some money. You know her father got locked up and left a bunch of that shit to her and her mother. I'd be stupid to not try and see what's really good with all that."

"Wait, so you telling me, you got plans on fuckin' with her even past what y'all just did? Can't you see how this is affecting me, JaMichael?" she asked, looking sick to her stomach.

"I ain't messing with her on that level, Tamia. I just wanna see what she's going to present before me, and we'll go from there. I ain't trying to hurt your feelings. I'm just trying to make shit happen for you, my sister, and Veronica. It's hard out here."

Tamia kept her head lowered and slowly began to shake it. Then tears fell from her eyes. "JaMichael, I'm asking you to never speak to that bitch again on the strength of me. Can you do that for me, baby? Please!" More tears came out of her eyes.

Seeing that got me choked up. Like I said before I hated to see a female cry, especially if I cared about them. I mean I didn't know if I would ever mess with Bubbie again, but I knew what Tamia needed to hear so I told her. I grabbed her to my body and wrapped her in my arms. "Yeah, Boo, you already know I will do anything for you. Bring yo' lil' emotional self over here."

"I just know that Bitch is up to no good. You're mine, and I don't want to share you," Tamia said, wrapping her arms around me, and nuzzling into my neck. I couldn't lie, she felt real good in my arms.

Chapter 12

I don't know how Bubbie got my number, but that night she blew my phone up, text after text saying how I needed to make sure, I got up with her as soon as possible. Out of respect for Tamia, I kept ignoring her messages. Mike-Mike hit me up first thing in the morning on some hustling shit. He didn't even give me enough time to get ready before he was outside Veronica's house blowing the horn. On my way out, I brushed past Jahliya, but I ain't say nothin' to her. She looked as if she wanted to say something to me, too, but instead, she held her silence. Probably from fear of us getting into an argument, so instead of speaking she simply kissed me on the cheek and smiled.

Her and Mikey seemed to be going pretty strong, I guess I still felt some type of way about all of that and I didn't know how to address it. A part of me was thinking sooner or later it was in my best interest to respect the fact that she was dating him. I mean after all she was my sister, and she was gon' do what she wanted to do anyway. Who was I to micromanage her steps in life?

When we got to the trap out in Black Haven it was already jumping. There was dope fiends lined up in front of our house, all the way down the sidewalk. I got inside and took a seat with a Ziploc bag full of raw and got to it. We had that Money Bagg banging in the background. So, while I got money, I couldn't help nodding my head as the fan blew directly on me.

The whole time I was working, Bubbie continued to blow up my phone with text after text. Finally, she started hitting up my Facebook. I ignored her messages until I offed my entire five-thousand-dollar pack. By that time, it was eight o'clock at night, and I ain't have shit to do any-way, so I hit her ass back.

She rolled to the trap literally fifteen minutes later and blew the horn to her whip. I strolled out and hopped into her truck. It smelled like perfume and restaurant food.

"I stopped over at, Blimpy's. I figured you'd be hungry after being in here trapping all day. I ain't know what kind of drink you like. I always see you drinking Vitamin waters at school, so I just got you one of them. She handed me a bag that looked like it was filled to the top.

I looked inside of it and frowned. "I ain't tell you to buy me no food. What you think you my lady or something?"

"N'all nigga, I ain't tryna be all that. Being somebody's lady come with too many restrictions. If anything, I'm just trying to be your close friend, and we can go from there. Do you have a certain time you gotta be home, or can we just roll for a minute?"

"We good, I'm finna fuck this food up. Then we gon' see what's on your mind." I said pulling out a fat ass, double cheeseburger, that was dripping with mayonnaise, and ketchup. I popped some curly fries into my mouth, hearing my stomach growl like a Lion.

"Damn, even I heard that over here. You must be hun-gry, huh?" She laughed and pulled a green Swisher from the console of her Jaguar truck. She placed the blunt in her mouth, sparked it, inhaled, and looked so fine to me. She took two pulls and blew the smoke out of her nose. "You wanna hit this shit? It's that bag." She held it out to me.

I was too busy chewing with my eyes closed. "Shorty you ain't bowling that bag." I couldn't help smacking.

"What's you got me messed up. That's all I blow is that thang." She jacked taking another pull. "But what make you say that, anyway, though?"

112

"Cause you ain't cop that shit from me." I twisted the cap off the Vitamin Water she'd brought for me.

She grunted and continued to drive. She rolled down her tinted window just a tad so the smoke could emit itself through the crack. "All I smoke is the best of the best. It's been like that ever since I started. You ain't hitting on shit, Playboy, at least not yet you ain't."

I laughed and continued to eat my food she'd purchased. "Not yet, huh? What you mean by that?"

"That means until you give me a spot in your life you gon' keep losing like you been doing. I got the Holy grail to this cash. All you gotta do is give me that chance. What you think 'bout that." She had her left eye squinted because the smoke constantly drifted up from the top of the blunt right into it. It seemed like no matter what she did she always looked so bad to me.

"Well, I'm here, right now. That means you got the perfect opportunity to put me up on whatever you need to. My ears are open. So is my stomach, too." I took another bite.

Bubbie drove for a little while in silence. She occasionally nodded her head to the music coming out of her speakers. She would look over at me and smile. Then go right back to driving. We musta been on the road for all of forty minutes before she pulled up to a small security tower. There she handed the older man her I.D. He looked it over, and looked down at her, before handing it back to her, and making the automatic black, metal gate slide to the side. We drove through it and entered onto a narrow path, that led into a wooded area. The wooded area turned into an arboretum. There was a pond on each side of the road. Then we were pulling up on a small hill that guided us directly to her mother's palace. When she pulled into the long driveway that was decorated by all kinds of expensive cars, and trucks. I would be lying if I said I wasn't impressed.

She cut the ignition, after parking behind a black on black Maserati. "Come on, JaMichael, let's go inside."

As soon as we stepped into the door, I was sizing up her crib. It was huge, and all white, with white statues of African Queens, situated in different places on the downstairs. There were expensive paintings on the wall as well. Her leather couches were white as well. It smelled real good. She kicked off her red bottom pumps and picked them up. When she bent over her black Gucci dress raised above her hips and clung to her thick thighs.

I peeped all of that and felt some type of way. I knew that before I left her crib, I was getting me some of what she had between her legs. She guided me through the house, explaining why her mother had purchased certain paintings. I half-listened and watched her ass jiggle under her dress, looking better and better.

Finally, we made it upstairs to her room, where she directed me inside. Her room was fit for a Princess. It was pink and white, clean, with a big vanity in the middle of it. She closed the door and went over to the computer where she put on some *H.E.R.* When she came back to the bed, she was nodding her head. I could tell she was feeling a whole lot better. She even had a smile on her pretty face.

"You can have a seat, JaMichael. Damn, you looking all awkward and shit." She laughed.

I had a choice of sitting on her couch or her bed. I chose to sit on her bed because that meant, I would be one step closer to tearing that ass up when it all came down to it.

She smiled and scooted next to me until our thighs were touching. Then she looked over at me. "JaMichael, I don't like seeing you walking back and forth like you are. I can tell you got that boss shit in you. You supposed to be riding something foreign, walking is for hoes." She leaned closer and kissed my neck, all sensual like.

I let her do all of that. "So, what you saying, you finna buy me a whip or something?" I leaned my head back so she could get a better grip with her lips on my neck.

She stopped and smirked. "Nigga, I don't think you know who you're fuckin' with. If you let me on your team, I'll make sure you pull away from my house tonight in a brand-new Benz. I'm talking black on black, with the red leather seats. I mean it ain't doing nothin' but just collecting dust in our driveway, anyway. My father ain't gon' be driving it no time soon. Somebody might as well drive it." She came around and straddled my lap.

Then she held my shoulders and looked me in the eyes. She was so fine that I looked off for a second, then summoned the courage to make it seem like she wasn't having an effect on me.

"Shorty did I tell you to sit yo' thick ass on my lap?" I asked, looking as serious as I could.

"I ain't gotta ask yo' permission for shit. You see how I'm living out here. Any real hustler gon' wanna live a life like this. Matter fact, that's my whole reason for calling you out here tonight. I wanna show you something." She kissed my lips and got off my lap.

I watched her walk out of the room, with her dress cuffing her ass. My phone buzzed. Tamia sent me a text asking me where I was? She said she missed me, and she wanted me to spend a night with her. As good as that sounded, I knew she wasn't trying to fuck, so I texted and told her I was hustling, and I would fuck with her later, or as soon as I was done getting money. She sent a sad face emoji, then

Bubbie walked into the room with a Burberry duffle bag in her hand.

She sat it on the bed and unzipped it. "Now don't get on no crazy shit wit' me, JaMichael. I'm only showing you this shit because I trust that you're more real than most of these game thugs out here. I wanna put you up on something but you gotta let me move at my own pace."

"No doubt, we can move however you wanna move. Long as the way you moving got something to do with us making some major cash. Does it?"

Bubbie pulled out a brick of Tar and sat it on the bed. "Look, this is just one of the many slabs I can show you."

I grabbed the bag from her and looked inside of it. There had to be about twenty more bricks of raw inside the bag. They were wrapped in aluminum foil and saran wrap. The aluminum foil had Chinese lettering on it and red dragons.

"Where the fuck you get all of this from?" I wanted to know.

She yanked the bag out of my hand. "It belongs to my father. But he can't do much with it seeing as he's in the feds now, can he?" She placed the strap of the bag over her shoulder and walked out of the room with it.

I wasn't the smartest man in the world when it came to yayo, but I knew for a fact, she had more than a million-dollars-worth of product in that bag. It took all of the willpower I had inside of me to not take it from her. Besides that robbing, a female shit wasn't in me no way. I knew there was a way I could finesse her out of the work. I just had to play my role.

When she came back into the room, she was carrying a bottle of Moët with the cork already popped. She took a sip out of the bottle and smiled that devilish ass smile. "I bet, I got your attention, now don't I?"

"Hell, yeah, you do." I walked over to her and pulled her into my warm embrace. "So, now that you don' shown me the merch. Does that mean you're about to put me on?" I asked kissing her neck. She smelled like perfume and hair care products.

"Mmm, that feels good. That may be what I had in mind. That all depends on what you're willing to do for me." She placed her hand in between our bodies and cuffed my dick. "I heard, Tamia bragging about how big your dick is. Then I saw, Mrs. Jamie deep throating this bad boy. She seemed like she was getting all that she could handle. Ja-Michael, I want you to tame my lil' ass. I don't care if I'm a lil' younger than you." She stepped on her tippy toes so she could suck on my neck.

I felt her hot tongue tracing the veins there. It felt so good I had to cuff her juicy ass. She moaned again and raised her dress above her waist. Now I was able to caress her flesh. I'd always known, Bubbie was thick, but a person couldn't get the most of how strapped she really was until they saw that ass in person like I was able to do. Since I knew she had all that dope in a bag in the house some-where, I dropped down and kissed the front of her panties, sniffing her box.

"Damn, Bubbie, I been feeling you for a long time. I just couldn't act on that shit because of my love for, Tamia. You know how that shit go though, Boo." I licked the front of her panties, I couldn't taste nothin' but cloth.

"Damn, you giving me the Boo title already? What I do to deserve that?" she asked, spacing her feet so I could get into her gap better.

I pulled them panties down her thighs and exposed her bald sex. She took a step back and placed a hand there to cover herself.

I was confused. "Fuck is you doing?"

Chapter 13

She wiggled out of her panties and tossed them carelessly on the floor, then she sat on the bed and opened her thighs wide enough for me to see that she didn't have any hair on her pussy. Her dark brown lips were puffy, they became darker the closer you got to the slit. I got on my knees in front of her, kissed her pussy, opened the lips and licked up and down her groove.

She dug her nails into my shoulders and tossed her head back. Her nipples were rock hard and poking through her dress. She squeezed her C-cup breasts together and continued to moan, while I ate her like Jahliya had taught me to do. After a while, I started enjoying eating her pussy. I think I was becoming obsessed with the act in general. I loved how it felt when a female buckled and moaned for me to keep going before they came all over my mouth. I felt empowered for some reason.

"Unhhh-unh-unhhh, JaMichael. Baby, it—feel—so—good! Fuck it do," she moaned, humping her fat cat into my face over and over again.

I took hold of her thighs and brought her face closer to me. Once there I was licking up and down her groove like crazy, trapping her clit, and sucking hard. I was chasing that duffle bag of raw that she had put up in that palace.

She arched her back and wrapped her ankles around my neck. *"JaMichael—JaMichael, oh my God! I'm cumming-I'm cumming, oh shit!"* she screamed at the top of her lungs, then fell back on the bed, shaking like crazy.

I kept on getting that cat, I made her open them thighs, and sucked all over them, licking up her juices. I was being mannish, and she was loving that shit. I scooted up on the bed beside her and pulled her right thigh open some more.

Then I was probing her slit, trying to see how deep my finger could go inside of her. From what I was seeing it wasn't that deep.

I leaned over and kissed her sex lips. "Uh, baby, you know my finger barely able to go in here, right?"

She moaned, "And what that's supposed to mean? Get up here and fuck me. I need some of you, right now."

I did what she asked, after pulling her dress all the way up and off. Her pretty nipples were huge, and the areola covered a nice portion of her breasts. They were dark circles that stood up like pacifiers. My tongue traced around each one, as she reached between our bodies and put my head right on her hole.

When I felt that heat all bets were off. She tensed and acted as if she was ready to run away from me, but I clung to her, and bucked forward, slamming deep into her body. Her pussy was tight and wet.

"*Oh shit, JaMichael!*" she hollered, digging her nails into my lower waist.

I sucked her neck as I long stroked that pussy over and over again. Her heat felt like it was searing me. She was so wet that our sex parts began to make slouching sounds. I pulled her to me and kept digging deeper and deeper, sucking, and nipping away at her neck.

When her thighs wrapped around me and she came. I couldn't help following suit. I came hard inside of her and kept right on stroking. Her pussy was good, it fit me like a glove. I'd be lying if I said, Jahliya didn't pop into my mind on more than a few occasions during our sex romp.

****

When it was all said and done, Bubbie laid her head on my thigh and gave me some of the best head of my young life. She held me in her fist and sucked only on the tip of my piece for five minutes, before bobbing up and down on nearly the whole thing. I came in her mouth, and she swallowed as much of me as she could, even though a nice portion came flowing back out. After she finished, she went and gargled with mouthwash before sliding back into the bed with me.

Almost immediately her right hand took a hold of my dick. "JaMichael, can I be honest with you about something?" she asked looking up at me.

Her room had a night light which allowed me to see her pretty eyes clearly. I was tired as hell, I knew I was staying out for the night. "Yeah, go ahead."

"I been feeling you ever since we were kids. I hated when you started going out with, Tamia. I just knew one day you was gon' wind up being my man, but that just never happened that way."

"You ain't never said nothin' to me. You was too busy acting all immature with, Tamia. Had you come at me like a woman, I would have given you some fuckin' wit. I mean, after all, you is bad as hell."

"Thank you, to be honest, I thought since you were messing with, Tamia, you wasn't going to give me the time of the day. I mean we both know she looks better than me, but if you ask me, I got the better body. At least that's what all of the boys say. But then again they probably tell her the same thing."

I rubbed down her back until I was cuffing that ass. It felt hot and soft in my hands. "Fuck them niggas opinions because they don't matter. The only one that matters is mine."

She was quiet for a second. "I agree. So, who do you think is harder? Me or Tamia, and be honest, don't just be saying that shit cuz' you're with me, right now."

"I ain't got no reason to sugarcoat shit. That ain't my speed, Shorty. I'm gon' always give that shit to you raw and uncut. You can take it however you want, that's on you."

"Okay, then who's badder in your opinion. Me or her?"

"Tamia overall finer, but you ain't that far behind. She just got a prettier face, and a lil more body than you do." Now in all honesty Bubbie was crushing Tamia on every level except the ass, but I couldn't let her know that because she was already used to niggas sweating her. I had to stay outside of them clowns or else her infatuation of me would fall off, I wasn't trying to lose that. Not until I had that bag in my hand.

"Dang, you ain't waste no time hurting my feelings. You coulda been a whole lot nicer," she said almost in a whisper.

I could tell that she was hurting, and of made me feel good. That meant I could penetrate her emotions. If I could penetrate her emotions, I could control her. There was dead silence in the room with the exception of the sound of the air conditioner.

"So, are you going to say you apologize for offending me or not?"

I slid my middle finger deep into her pussy. "Shorty, hell n'all, you asked me a question. I told you the truth. If you can't handle that shit, then you shouldn't have asked me to keep it real with you. That's just that."

"But you really think she looks better than me, though?" she sounded wounded.

I pulled her lil' ass further up until she had her head laying directly over my heart. I held her firmly. "Not by

122

much. You're still a badass female. I wouldn't just lay up with anybody. You're the only female that tempt me in the way that you do. I love, Tamia, I shouldn't be doing this shit." I made it seem like I was about to get up out of the bed.

She held me down and straddled my lap. "Fuck that, JaMichael, I want you to be with me. I'll take you to the top. I got everything you need right here in this house. I'll make sure you be shitting on these Memphis niggas in a matter of months. Facts!"

I wanted to smile but I had to stay in character. "Oh, yeah, Bubbie. How is you going to do that?"

She hopped out of the bed and rushed out of the room. While she was out I checked my phone. I had ten texts from Tamia, and four from Jahliya worrying about where I was. Bubbie came back into the room carrying a kilo. She tossed it on the bed next to me.

"Huh, all you gotta do is to make me your side bitch for, right now while you get yourself together. I won't cause no drama or be beefing with your main bitch. I'ma just stay in my lane and be there when you need me to be. But in return whenever I need you, I'ma need you to get to me as soon as possible. Does that sound like a deal?"

I looked the brick over in my hands. "That sound like a hell of a deal. Now give me some information on this work, how good is it?"

Bubbie shrugged her shoulders. "I really don't know too much about that stuff. All I know is that my father got rich off this same dope. He was cracking for years, and he has a ton of it left. If you mess with me, I'll keep it steady for you. He loves me, and he'll give me anything I want. It's always been that way with him."

I still couldn't believe she had given me a whole ass bird. I felt like Bubbie was a gold mine. I needed to keep her close. Not only for the financial beneficial side of things, but also because she was bad, and I just liked having a badass bitch around me. I knew Tamia was going to make things difficult, but I would cross that bridge when I came to it.

****

Jahliya was waiting up on her bed in our room when I got home early the next morning. She looked tired and real irritated. I walked past her and gave her a faint hello. I was tired and exhausted. I wanted to steal an hour of sleep before I had to get to school. I could feel her staring a hole into my face, so I tried my best to avoid making eye contact with her.

"Since when we stop answering each other's texts, especially the ones in the wee hours of the night? Obviously, showing concern about the other person's safety?"

I set my alarm for one hour, threw on an outfit, and laid out on my back on my bed. I had already showered at Bubbie's crib. "Man, I was handling something. Then by the time I was finished I was so tired I passed out. She had to wake me up early this morning or I woulda still been lying in her bed, right now." I closed my eyes and tried desperately to pass out.

"Aw, so you was with some bitch last night, huh?" Jahliya snapped.

"Yeah! Why? That make you feel some type of way or something?"

"Aw n'all, you damn near grown, JaMichael. You can do whatever you wanna do. I just know the next time I hit

124

you up worrying about your ass, you better be hitting me back to let me know you are alive. Do you understand me?"

"Jahliya, do you understand the concept of a mafucka setting they alarm for an hour? That means they are trying to get an hour of sleep. If I stay up arguing with yo' lil' ass for the whole hour, then I set the clock for nothing." I smiled and tried to doze off.

Jahliya came over and smacked me on my chest with an open hand. It hurt like a muthafucka. My sister may have been small, but she was heavy-handed as hell.

I sat up, furious. "Man, what the fuck is wrong with you?"

She stood at the edge of the bed, furious. She paced back and forth and kept clenching and unclenching her fists. She had a habit of doing this whenever she got mad. "JaMichael, you had me up worried about your ass all night. I didn't know what the fuck happened, but I couldn't help expecting the worst. Damn, I was so fuckin' worried about you. I can't imagine being in this world without you. I don't give a fuck how mad I get with you, you're all I have." She covered her face with her hands and broke down.

I jumped right up and pulled her into my arms. I tried to move her hands from her face, but she wouldn't let me. So, instead, I held her and started to kiss the back of her hands. "I'm sorry, sis. I'm sorry, I was bugging. I'll never do you like that again, I promise."

"You can't be doing shit like that to me, JaMichael." She hit me on the shoulder, then wrapped her arms around my waist. She rested her head on my chest. "It shouldn't be no bitch in this world that'll stop you from getting be back to me. I don't care if you're knee-deep in her pussy. You are to make me a muthafuckin' priority. Do you hear me?"

125

I nodded. "Yeah, I hear you Jahliya, now calm down." I kissed her on the top of the head and held her.

She allowed for me to keep her securely within my embrace, before she stepped backward out of them, and looked into my eyes. Her cheeks were tear-streaked. She stood on her toes, grabbed the back of my neck and brought my face to hers. Our lips kissed, then she was sliding her tongue into my mouth, moaning into it.

I couldn't help grabbing her ass and kneading it like dough. I pulled her closer to me, broke our kiss, and was all over her neck. She moaned louder, slipped her hands down my pants and took a hold of my dick. "JaMichael, I can't lose you, baby. I can't lose you, you're all I have. I can't let nobody take you away from me." She broke away, closed the bedroom door, pulled her blouse over her head, and dropped her skirt. She walked back over to me in just a pair of bikini panties. I could see her camel toe as clear as day. It looked good. When she got in from of me, she took a hold of my dick again. "Do you want me, Ja-Michael? Do you want me more than that bitch's house you just left?"

I grabbed her and sucked on her neck some more. My hand slid under her bra and tweaked her nipple. She tossed her head back and moaned out loud, "JaMichael, I need to hear you tell me you want me more than you want her. Please tell me," she whispered, her voice was heavy with lust.

I picked her lil' ass up and she wrapped her thighs around me. I crashed into the wall with her. "You already know I do." I sucked harder on her neck. "Stop asking me that stupid ass question." We fell on the bed with me on top of her.

Her ankles interlocked around my waist. My dick was throbbing so hard, it felt like it was trying to break through my boxers. She humped up from the bed and groaned deep within the back of her throat when she felt me throbbing against her.

"I want you too, JaMichael! I swear to God I want you, too!" She reached in between us and took a hold of my dick again. She rubbed me up and down her slit, over the panties. The material was so wet, I could feel her heat as clear as day. She got up and stood on the side of the bed, pulled her bikini panties down, and stepped out of them. "I know what it's gon' take to lock yo' ass down. I can't have you putting these other hoes over me. I know what you want, so come on, and let's do this." She climbed onto the bed and crawled across it with her ass in the air.

I could see her cat from the back. It looked puffy, and it glistened. I stood there on rock hard, wanting to cross those lines with her, but knowing I could not. She looked good to me. Like forbidden fruit, or the last slice of pizza that a person knew they weren't supposed to have for whatever reason. The more I looked at her the more excited I became.

She finally laid on her side, and slid her hand between her thighs, caressing her pussy. "Come on baby, bruh, let's just get this shit over with. Once we do it, we've done it, and we can see how it'll make us feel."

I shrugged my shoulders. I couldn't turn Jahliya down as much as I wanted too. I kneeled on the bed with my piece in my hand and all of a sudden Veronica started beating on the door. We scrambled to get dressed.

"Jahliya, that damn boy outside with that loud ass music. Go out there and tell him to turn that shit down before he gets me put out!" she hollered, ruining our mood, and knocking us out of our forbidden lustful zone.

Chapter 14

I took the brick, Bubbie gave me and split it down the middle with Getty. He had this spot over on Melrose, right down the street from Orange Mound. Melrose was known for having all the heroin addicts. Our Trap was located right in the middle of the block. Getty hadn't had it open for more than three hours before we were going hard. It seemed like as soon as the fiends heard we were in business, and the shop was open, they couldn't get to us fast enough. They lined up in an orderly fashion to receive our product: five, ten, and twenty dollars at a time. While Getty was serving the fiends and foiling up the work, I would multi-task, and be doing my homework as well.

There were only a few weeks of school left, and graduating was definitely a focal point for me. Even though I was living in the hood, I always thought outside of the hood. I wanted to make movies one day, but before then I wanted to write a book about the slums of Memphis. I had no idea what I would call it, but I knew I wanted to write one.

One Friday afternoon while we were bagging up a quarter-brick, Getty stopped and looked over at me. "Say, JaMichael, I don't know if you know it or not, but we got people looking for us. One of the homies from Black Haven told me some niggas were rolling around in a black on black Excursion truck asking questions. I don't know what's really good, but we gotta be prepared for everything. I want you to carry this on your hip at all times, and if anything looks funny, you betta pop this bitch until yo' clip run empty," he said, passing me a black .40 Glock.

I looked it over, the first thing I noted was the weight of it. "Getty, what's good with that fool, Parker? Wouldn't he be able to tell you who supposed to be looking for us, if it's anybody at all?" I needed to know. I'd had a bad feeling about Parker, ever since things went down in Nashville.

Getty stood up and took his latex gloves off. "I think Parker might be a serious problem. He done sent me a few texts saying I gotta meet him in Nashville for an important meeting, but I been snubbing his ass. I think he trying to set me up." He pulled a blunt out of his pocket and set fire to it.

I cocked the .40 and aimed at a spot. "So, why we ain't put that fool down the night that all of this shit happened? Seems like he can give these niggas the green light to come and sweat us whenever they feel like it. What type of shit is that?"

Getty sat on the couch of the trap. There was about two thousand dollars on the table in front of him. He began counting it bill by bill as if he was trying to buy time to give me a response.

"Well, nigga?" I was getting irritated because I felt like we'd made the wrong decision, to begin with trusting, Parker. It seemed like he had more loyalty to Screw and his people than he did Getty. I was confused as to why Getty would trust him to begin with.

"That nigga like family, Joe. Had I known that shit was about to go down like this, maybe I would have played things differently. But then again, we don't even know for sure if it was, Parker that was rolling around the Mound. It coulda been the other nigga that wound up getting away. Shit just crazy, right now." He lowered his head and took a pink Sprite out of his bookbag, he carried with him.

I didn't know what to say. A part of me wanted to chew him out because of his decision making, but I had to remember both me and the homie were young niggas, and we were just starting to figure the game out. I went back to foiling up my work, and an hour later we reopened the Trap and served the addicts until three in the morning.

****

Jahliya came and picked me up from Getty's trap at about three-thirty. She was rolling a money green Lexus fresh off the lot. When I came downstairs and saw her sitting on the hood of the whip, the first thing I became was jealous.

"Who the fuck car is this?" I grumbled, embracing her on the sidewalk.

She looked nervous. "Aw, this is my birthday present from, Phoenix."

"*Phoenix*, why the fuck would he give you a brand new Lexus? And your birthday ain't until next month," I added, making a revolution around the car. That boy was clean and shining as if she'd just gotten it waxed.

"I think, Phoenix, got a thing for me too because every time, Mikey turn his back he's always giving me something, like this." She pulled a bundle of cash out of her purse and held it up for me to see.

I ignored the cash and got into the passenger's seat. I didn't like them niggas doing shit for my sister. The reason I had been out trapping all night was so I could make sure she was straight all across the board. I had a thousand dollars I was going to give her just because, but after seeing the bundle of cash she was toting, I decided against it.

She climbed inside of her whip and placed the key in the ignition. Before she turned it on, she looked over at me with a solemn expression on her face. "Are you okay, baby brother?"

I shook my head. "I just don't like these niggas doing all this shit for you. I don't need no help in providing for us. I'm figuring shit out, I'll have things put together sooner or later."

Jahliya rested her hand on my thigh. "But you don't have to place our situation solely on your shoulders. We are supposed to be a team. You and I, we have to look out for each other. We are all that we have. It's always been that way." She started the car and pulled away from the curb.

"Man, I just love you, Jahliya. When I imagine another nigga trying to do for you what I am more than capable of doing, it simply irritates my soul. I feel like sooner or later you're going to start loving that nigga Mikey, and you gon' wind up choosing him over me. That's gon' be the worst day of my life, I'm just keeping shit real."

Jahliya kept on driving. "JaMichael, I don't even know how you could say something like that? How could you ever think I could love one of these niggas more than you? Haven't I proven to you that you mean more than anybody in this world to me?"

I nodded. "Yeah, you have, but when you're worried about losing somebody, Jahliya none of that shit comes into a person's mind. All I see is these niggas doing shit for you that I ain't able to do, right now. Don't you think, I'd love to be able to cop you a brand new Lexus fresh off the lot?"

"I know you would, JaMichael, but why would you have too if I got these other niggas to do it?"

"Because I need to, sis. I need to know that you will never ever need another dude outside of me. Every time I see one of them doing something for you that I can't, that shit just makes me feel so insecure."

132

Jahliya shook her head. "JaMichael, I'm your big sister. You're not supposed to feel less than a man because you can't take care of me. I'm supposed to feel that way because I can't take care of you."

"Fuck that, a man's job is to take care of the women inside of his household. That's how it's supposed to be," I said, trying to calm myself down because I was getting riled up.

Jahliya smiled. "Who taught you that, JaMichael?"

"Ain't nobody teach me that. It's instilled inside of me, and I know what's right, and what's wrong. It's wrong for any nigga to be out here getting money, and not take care of the women under his roof. Matter of fact we're moving out of Veronica's shit, and into our own place at the end of this month. I think it's time we did that."

Jahliya was quiet for a few blocks. I thought I had said something wrong. "I got something I gotta tell you, Ja-Michael."

"What's that? I hope it ain't no bad news."

"N'all, it's nothin' like that, but Mikey copped me this lil' spot over on Washington Avenue. It's a condo and looks really nice. Three bedrooms, one and a half bath, and a view of the skyline. I'm supposed to move in at the end of this month. I was going to tell you in the morning."

I was caught off guard and immediately became angry. "Fuck, this nigga supposed to be living wit' you or something now?" I snapped.

"No."

"He buying you a crib so he can control you. That nigga got a plan for you, and you don't even know it. I'm letting you know this shit, right now, if I ever even think that dude bitch ass trying to harm you in any way, I'm smoking him. And I'ma start knocking them Duffle Bag Cartel niggas off one by one. I'm not gon' play about you, Jahliya. I mean that shit with every fiber of my being. That's on my mother. Rest in peace!"

Jahliya took a deep breath and blew it out slowly. "Damn, Jam, why the fuck you have to be my brother? You would make the best man for any woman if you loved them as much as you loved me. Damn!" She shook her head. "I ain't gon' let that nigga play me. Your sister got more swag than you give me credit for. I see how they play them other hoes every single day. They don't try and pull that shit with me, though. Mikey ain't even fucked yet, shit ain't sweet." She rolled to the red lights and stopped.

"Yet, huh? That means, he'll be getting some sooner or later. It's only a matter of time."

Jahliya remained silent, as she tapped her fingers on the steering wheel, and looked both ways, before grabbing her cup of Pop from the console. One of her shoulder straps fell off her shoulder and revealed the top of her right breast. It looked good to me. The light turned green and just as she was about to pull off a black minivan pulled up alongside us, and two dudes with shotguns jumped out of the side of it and aimed their weapons at her window.

"Bitch, get the fuck out of the car, right now!" one hollered.

I was surprised that they were doing this shit without a mask on their faces.

Jahliya frowned. "Fuck is y'all robbing people in your own community for? Take that shit to the suburbs."

The same robber knocked on the glass with the barrel of his weapon. "Bitch, I ain't gon' tell you again. Get the fuck out of the car of I'm finna blow yo' shit back."

"Jahliya, get out of the car, sis. Fuck them, let 'em have this mafucka," I advised.

She shot daggers at me. "Fuck them, JaMichael. This is my car, I just got it. Phoenix ain't even put no insurance on it yet."

The second robber pumped his shotgun. He aimed it at me through the windshield. "Get the fuck out of the car, homeboy."

"Jahliya, we getting out! Don't say another mutha-fuckin' word. Just get yo' ass out of the car," I said holding my hands up after opening the door a lil' bit.

Jahliya finally complied, she opened the door and stepped into the night. "You pussy ass niggas need to get a fuckin' job. What type of niggas are out robbing people from their community at damn near four in the—"

The first robber swung and knocked her cleanout. As soon as he dropped her, he stomped her three times in the stomach. I could hear her holler out in pain. It was the worst thing that I had ever heard. He raised his foot to stomp her again, and I don't know how I managed to get to it so fast, but the next thing I knew, I had the .40 in my hand and was firing shot after shot. The first and second one ripped through his neck and made him spin before he fell to the ground twisting on the pavement.

His guy must have been caught off guard because he nearly tripped over his foot as he let off a shot and dropped the shotgun on the concrete. Their van sped away. The second robber took off running. I chased him for a second, then I stopped in the middle of the street, and fired back to back. I could literally see the holes fill up his back before he fell face first in the street. Then I was rushing around the Lexus, and stuffing Jahliya into the back seat of it. She continued to groan. I could sense she was in some excruciating pain. I jumped behind the steering wheel and stormed away from the curb.

Chapter 15

Two weeks later, Jahliya had yet to recover. The first robber had broken three of her ribs and blackened her eye. It made me feel sick on the stomach, I even cried. I had vowed to never allow my sister to be hurt. I'd actually allowed her to be hurt right in front of me. I felt like a pussy, I felt weak, like I had no purpose in life. I couldn't even look her in the eyes anymore. I couldn't help wondering if she looked at me the same. It was a question I wanted to ask her, but I didn't think I was strong enough to accept her response if it wasn't the response I was looking for.

In the third week, her ribs were finally healing, and she wasn't experiencing as much pain. I'd fallen into a major state of depression over that night. Not only was I feeling like a failure for failing to protect her, but the two dudes I'd smoked were haunting me. I say haunt because I kept seeing them in my nightmares. They kept asking me why I'd killed them, then they would pull me down into this fiery pit and start screaming like lil' a little girl at recess who was being chased. I had seen the two robbers in my dreams every night since the shootings took place.

One night, Jahliya woke up to find me sitting on the edge of my bed with tears streaming down my face. I was tired of being haunted. I was tired of not being able to sleep through the night. On top of that I knew, I had failed my sister. I was so depressed, I was contemplating suicide, it was that bad.

When Jahliya awoke, she turned on the lamp and saw my tears she went into action. "Aw baby what's the matter?" She got up, sat next to me, and placed her arm around my shoulders. "Talk to me, JaMichael now," she demanded.

I didn't know what to say, I had never cried in front of my sister as a young man. The fact that I was doing it this day made me feel some type of way.

"I'm sick, sis. I keep seeing them bitch ass niggas that did this shit to you. I keep seeing you being assaulted in the street. I keep having bad dreams that they are haunting me and asking me why I killed them. This shit is killing my soul so much, I have been thinking about taking my life."

Jahliya hopped up and closed the bedroom door that I didn't even notice was open until she closed it. Then she came and stood in front of me. "What the fuck you just say?"

"You heard me, sis. This shit is starting to mess with my mental. I can't think, I can barely eat. I don' lost nine pounds already."

"So, what does that have to do with you killing yourself?" she asked, frowning.

That got me defeated. The last thing I needed was a lecture from her. "You know what, just forget about it. I don't want to talk about this shit no more. Let me try and get some sleep." I slid under the covers and got ready to pull them over my head when she stopped me.

"Look, JaMichael, I'm sorry." She exhaled and gingerly eased onto my bed. "Can you sit up with me for a minute?" she asked, rubbing my chest.

That softened me, I sat up and kept my eyes closed. For some reason, I was experiencing the worst migraine I had ever had in all of my life. "What's good, sis?"

She took my hand and placed it on her thighs, then began rubbing the top of it. "Lil' bro, I need you to holla at me, Mane. Tell me what's really going on. I'm here for you." She went from rubbing my hand, to rubbing my back.

I lowered my head. "Sis, it really ain't shit. I just been seeing these niggas I hit up over you. I feel like they are haunting me. In addition to that, I feel like I dropped the ball protecting you. That shit ain't sitting right wit' me. I see what happened to you every time I close my eyes. I failed you. That's what's good with me."

"But bro', you did everything you possibly could. You took those niggas lives for me. They ain't breathing no more. If you wouldn't have stepped in, that man was getting ready to kill me, and you're sitting here thinking you failed me? Boy, stop it." She wrapped her arm around my neck and kissed my cheek. "I love you, JaMichael. I already know you crazy about me. You prove that to me every single day. You don't need to be in here shedding tears, Ernest. I feel like you saved my life that night. I am forever indebted to you because of that."

I hated when she called me Ernest, it happened ever so often. Ernest was the name my mother Blaze had given me, it was her father's name. She'd originally named me August Ernest Stevens, but when me and Jahliya were adopted by Veronica when I was just two years old, she'd changed my name to JaMichael, and allowed my middle name to remain the same. I never found out why she changed it, and I honestly didn't care.

"It's all good, Jahliya. I was just going through something. You know how that shit go, I'll be alright real soon." I stood up and ran my hands over my face. "I gotta bounce back, I'll be a'ight, though."

She came from behind me and slid her arms past my neck until her hands were resting on my chest. "You're a rider for me, JaMichael. I knew you was crazy about me. I just want you to know, I would do anything for you as well. But I'ma show you better than I can tell you. I don't see no other nigga but you. I don't care about no man in this world other than you. I need you to know this, JaMichael because I mean it with all of my soul." She hugged me and kissed the back of my neck. It felt so good.

I turned around, pulled her to me, kissed her cheek, and then her lips. It was only a peck, then I was holding her for dear strength. We stayed that way for what seemed like a full hour, though it had only been minutes. "We gotta get out of here, sis. We gotta get our own lil' spot. It's time we leave, Veronica's nest."

"I move in a few weeks, you already know you are more than welcome to come along. In fact, I'ma need you around just to keep me safe, and sound." She kissed me again and hugged my body. "I love you so much, Ja-Michael, I mean so-so much."

I picked her up and allowed her to wrap her thighs around me while I held her in the air, before falling on the bed with her. "I told you I'd kill a nigga over you with no hesitation. You're mine, Jahliya, I mean that shit."

She snuggled closer to me and kissed my lips. "I already know that I swear I do. Come on, just hold me for a few hours."

****

Getty woke me up sometime that night by beating on our bedroom window. Jahliya jumped up first, seemed to be spooked. She dropped the floor and laid on her stomach as if she was expecting shots to rain out. By me being paranoid and thinking something wasn't right, instead of going directly to the window to see what was good. I ran out the back door to the house, and along the gangway, until I came to where he was standing on a milk crate trying to see into

140

the window. The .40 Glock was aimed directly to send a slug through the back of his head. I wasn't about to play no games. When he looked and saw that it was me, he threw his hands in the air. "JaMichael, what the fuck is you doing nigga?"

I rushed him and kept my gun trained on him all the way until I was in his face. "Nigga fuck is you doing beating on that window like that? You know what the fuck happened to my sister already. Are you out of your mind?"

Getty kept his hands up. "Damn, nigga, that's my fault. I wasn't thinking, but I gotta holla at you like asap. We got a problem, I'm talking a serious problem."

I lowered the gun and had to take a second so my heart could stop beating so fast. I was amped up and still mad as hell. My last sight of Jahliya before I left the room was of her up shaking like a leaf. I didn't like no mafucka scaring my sister. I didn't care who they were. I waved for Getty to follow me to the back of the house, but before we went back there, I stood on the crate and told Jahliya everything was okay. That it was only, Getty. She nodded to me and sat on the bed with her arms wrapped around her knees.

Getty was pacing back and forth when I got to the backyard. The moonlight shined from the sky. There was a light drizzle of rain falling. I ignored it and penned my eyes on Getty.

"Bitch nigga named, Grizzly at us, JaMichael."

"Who the fuck is, Grizzly?"

"That's Screw's brother. You know the nigga we had to hit up for that work a few weeks back. I guess his brother Grizzly just rolled into town from South Carolina. And you ain't gon' believe what they did to that fool, Parker." He shook his head and continued pacing.

The wind picked up speed just a bit. I didn't have a shirt on, so I was freezing. "What they do to him?"

"Well, I don't know how true it is, but what was told to me by Parker's cousin Mick, was that Parker's arms and legs were cut off one by one, and they fed them bitches to the alligators. That's fucked up. I heard that nigga, Grizzly got a real sadistic ass reputation. Now that nigga talking about, he wanna meet with me, so he can figure out what took place that night."

I bucked my eyes. "And you finna go and holla at him?"

"Hell, n'all, that's why I came over here tonight. I think it'll be in our best interest if we go at him first. If we wait around for him to get at us, shit gon' be real fucked up. Ain't no telling what fate we might meet. At least by going at his chin, we are in control of our own destiny."

I was hugging myself now because I was so cold. "Damn, man, it's always something. Do that fool know where you lay yo head?"

Getty shrugged his shoulders. "I can't be sure. If they fucked over Parker like his cousin is saying they did, it just ain't no telling what he told them before they finished him off. Like I said, Grizzly been rolling around Memphis looking for us. So, I'm guessing if he had my address, he woulda came directly to me instead of rolling around trying to find out where I was."

"Shit this is fucked up. Do he got a bunch of niggas wit' him? Like where they from?" I asked freezing. I was ready to go into the house.

"Screw's people fuck around heavy in Texas. This nigga, Grizzly is from South Carolina. I don't how they get down out that way, but I can only imagine they hittas. I mean why else would they travel all the way to Memphis on bidness?"

"Where is he, right now?" I looked over my shoulder as a car rolled down the street with its trunk knocking.

I was getting paranoid. Not only was I worried about the repercussions coming from the situation that happened with Jahliya. Now I had to worry about the Nashville hit. I couldn't even enjoy the fact that I had graduated from high school with a three-point-five grade point average.

"I don't know where he's at for a fact, but as soon as I find out I'm coming to get you, and we gon' handle our bidness. We can't let this nigga hunt us, we gotta hunt his ass. That's just how shit goes, survival of the deadliest." He extended his hand. "You fuckin' wit' me right?"

I shook up and pulled him to me. "Nigga, I'm fuckin' wit' you the long way. I'm all in like Poker Chips."

"That's all I needed to hear. I'ma get on up out of here, I'll be in touch. Oh, and this is yours." He went into his pocket and came up with two thousand in cash. "I stayed up all night trapping. This is your cut from the bag I rocked."

I nodded. "Good looking, bruh."

We hugged, and parted ways. All I could think about was the fact that my life was on the line. I didn't even know the people that were trying to get at me. To say that I was worried was an understatement.

****

When I got back inside Jahliya was sitting g on the floor with her arms wrapped around her knees. She had her chin resting on her knees. I sat beside her and pulled her to me. "You okay, Jahliya?"

She shook her head. "I was scared, JaMichael. I was scared that we were under attack. I keep seeing that somebody is going to take you away from me. I couldn't handle that, JaMichael, losing you would kill me. I need you in this world. Nothing makes sense if you ain't here with me." She broke into tears.

I felt my throat get tight immediately. I hated when my sister cried. I felt like the world was coming to an end, there was tears coming down her cheeks. "Jahliya, I'm good, baby. I love you too much to allow anybody to take you away from me, or me away from you. You are my heart and soul. Everything I do, I do for you. Now stop shedding these tears. You know I can't handle that shit."

This only made her cry harder. "I keep seeing it in my dreams, JaMichael. Somebody kills you, and I'm at your funeral with my head hung low, balling my eyes out. Then as soon as your funeral is over, I kill myself because I can't live without you. I say we get the fuck out of Memphis. It's our only hope for survival, I'm telling you."

"Sis, we gotta get a lot more paper than we got, besides, Memphis is home. I'm not about to have nobody chasing me from my homeland. That ain't happening, I got us though. We'll be okay." I kissed her forehead. "You trust me don't you?"

She nodded. "Yeah, I do, I just wish I didn't keep having these dreams. Come on, let's go to sleep. I need you to hold me all night and do not let me go. I'm begging you."

I did exactly what she asked. I wound up laying in the bed with Jahliya for two days straight. During this time, she continued to break down telling me about the nightmares she was having about somebody taking my life. Her dreams caused me to become a bit fearful. I had so much going on that I honestly felt it was only a matter of time before one, or a bunch of things caught up to me.

Chapter 16

"I just wanna know why it seems like you've been avoiding me? You haven't answered any of my texts, or Facebook messages in nearly two weeks. Was it something I did?" Tamia asked while she sat across from me at Dee's cafe. She looked as if she were near tears. Her voice kept breaking up, and she'd taken more than one deep breath.

Dee's cafe was one of the hot spots in Memphis for teenagers. Most teens kicked it there when they wanted to meet up with their friends, or just to be around other teens in general. Dee's specialized in double cheeseburgers, and classic vanilla milkshakes. I'd agreed to go here with Tamia so we could talk and already it seemed as if she was getting emotional. I had so much shit on my mind that I knew it was going to be hard to go there mentally with her, but I was going to try.

"Shorty, I been busy trying to get my shit together. You know me and Jahliya are finally moving into our own place at the end of this week." I ate one of my curly fries and chased it down with a vanilla milkshake. It tasted good as hell.

"So, that stops you from getting back to me?" She looked into my eyes and reached across the table to rest her hand on top of mine.

"N'all, it ain't been nothin' like that. I just been trying to get my priorities in order. I gotta make sure my sister is straight at all times. That's all that is."

"So, basically what you're saying is that she is all that matters." She crossed her arms in front of her Coogi dress. She had her hair curled so it bounced every time she moved in the slightest.

I slid around to her side of the booth, put my arm around her shoulder and kissed her warm cheek. "N'all, boo, once again, I ain't saying it like that. What I'm saying is that my sister done been through some shit. For the last few weeks, I been taking care of her because that's my job. I know I been neglecting you, and I really don't mean to. I'm sorry, and you still mean the world to me."

She smiled and laid her head on my chest. "Thank you for saying that. Now if you acted that way, we would be all good."

I laughed her statement off and went back to eating my food. The door to Dee's cafe opened, and something told me to look up. When I did, I saw Bubbie walk through the door with Phoenix. He had his arm around her and was whispering something in her ear. She laughed, nodded, then looked over to see me. At the sight of me, she froze and removed his arm from around her neck.

"Aw shit, here go this punk ass bitch," Tamia uttered, shifting uncomfortably.

Phoenix walked up to the counter to order their food, and Bubbie walked over to us. She looked down on me and smiled ignoring Tamia. "Hey, JaMichael, how have you been?"

I nodded. "I been good, been taking care of my sister. What's been good with you?"

Tamia perked up. "Uh, what the fuck is going on here? How the fuck did y'all get all friendly and shit?"

Bubbie was rocking a Givenchy dress that clung to her curves like a second skin. I could tell she didn't have a bra on because her areolas were prominent and sticking up against her outfit. She smiled and popped back on her legs. Even from where I sat, I could see her ass cheeks jiggle with the sudden movement. "You wanna tell her what's up, or should I?"

Tamia frowned and looked over at me. "Fuck is she talking about, JaMichael?"

I shrugged my shoulders. "I don't know what the fuck she talking about. She sounds like she tripping, though."

Bubbie looked offended. "Tripping, aw that's how you finna play me, JaMichael? You finna play me like this because you fucking wit' this bum ass bitch? A'ight then." She nodded her head.

Phoenix slid up alongside her and placed his arm around her shoulders. "You ready to order your food lil', Momma?" He nodded '*what up*' to me.

Bubbie removed herself from under him. "JaMichael, I need to talk to you for a minute."

Tamia stood up. "Bitch, you don't think fat meat is greasy, do you? You gon' sit here and keep trying to come at my man like I'm not right in front of y'all? Fuck you think it's sweet or something?"

Bubbie laughed again. "Bitch first of all yousa bum. If you talking like you wanna fight me, I'll just pay a Bitch to get all in yo ass. I'm sure one of these hoes in here would love to make a quick thousand dollars to get all in yo' ass like booty hair. I refuse to break a nail on yo' nobody ass."

Tamia scooted her chair out of the way and made her way around the table. She stood in Bubbie's face and clenched her teeth. "Bitch, you think you're all of that because you got a few pennies put up? Pennies that your father had to give his life for."

Bubbie bumped her chest into Tamia. "Bitch, you don't know nothing about my father. You only know what the streets say, and they don't know nothin' either. It's in your best interest to keep him out of your vocabulary."

Tamia pointed her finger at Bubbie's head. "Bitch fuck you. You ain't running shit. I'll whoop you, and any other bitch that want some if y'all trying to fuck in my bidness. Ain't no hoes over here."

I stood up and separated the two of them. Phoenix had a big smile on his face. "Man, you better grab lil' shorty before my lil' cousin gets all up in her ass, straight up," he jacked.

"Man, they ain't finna fight over here. I ain't about to let that shit ride," I said pulling Tamia behind me.

"Yeah, you better hold me back. I'll stomp a mudhole in that hoe, believe that," Tamia snapped.

Once again Phoenix laughed, then he placed his arm around Bubbie's shoulder. "Come and order your food, Bubbie. Then we gon' get the fuck up out of here a'ight."

Bubbie allowed herself to be led away for a few feet, then she came from under Phoenix's arm. "Fuck that, I need to holla at you for a minute. Just step outside for a second so we can talk. After we holla, I'll leave you and your girl alone."

"Bitch I'm still trying to find out what you need to talk to my man so bad about? I ain't wit' all that secretive shit. If you got anything to say to him, you can say that shit right in front of me. Ain't that right, baby?" she said this looking back to me.

I didn't know what to say or do. Phoenix had a big ass smile on his face, that irritated me to my very core. I was a bit tongue-tied. Since it took me so long to make a decision.

Tamia exhaled loudly. "Damn, okay, I see what it is then. A'ight, JaMichael, gon' head and holla at her, I'll see you in the car." She bumped Bubbie, before heading to the parking lot.

"Y'all finna holla then I'ma gon' head and give y'all your space," Phoenix said, looking down at Bubbie to see what she was going to say.

Bubbie nodded. "Yeah, gon' head and do you for a minute. Me and JaMichael have unfinished bidness." She looked into my eyes and took hold of my hand.

Tamia saw this, and her eyes became watery. She rushed out of the restaurant and into the parking lot. I felt bad for her, but obviously, Bubbie didn't. She waved her off, led me through the kitchen, and out of the back door that led to some stairs. We went up them and stopped in front of an apartment door that I never knew existed.

"Shorty where the fuck are you taking me?" I asked, watching my back.

She took a key out of her pocket and placed it inside the lock. "Be cool, my aunt is Dee, she owns this cafe, and this lil' apartment right here is mine." She unlocked the door and pushed it in.

The apartment was small and cozy. It had a three-piece black leather couch set, with a glass table, and a huge 4K television on the wall. It smelled like Jasmin. She made me take off my shoes before leading me inside where we gathered on the couch.

Once there she leaned over and kissed my lips. "I've missed you so much, baby. I'm sorry for getting down on 'ol girl, but when I saw how y'all were all hugged up and shit that made me feel some type of way. I see how overprotective I am over you. Are you mad at me?"

I shook my head. "N'all, you good shorty. I know you got me in a bunch of bullshit with her, but I'll deal with that shit at another time. What's so important that we had to meet in person?"

"Before we get to that. How are things going with the packages I gave you?" She kissed my necks and sat on my lap.

"They good, I'm doing what I supposed to do with 'em. Getting this money like I supposed to do. Why, are you worried about something?"

She shook her head. "Oh, I'm not worried about anything. If I was worried about something you would have known already." She licked my earlobe. "But just for the sake of argument how much money do you have ready for me?"

"Shit, right now. My sister got beat up real bad, I had to handle some bidness. Niggas tried to rob her, and it was crazy. I ain't been hustling like I really want, too. I'm back at that shit first thing in the morning."

Bubbie nodded her head. "You saying your sister got beat up real bad. Why you ain't telling me about the part where you killed both of them niggas that tried to rob her?"

When she said this shit a chill went down my spine. "Fuck is you talking about, Bubbie?"

"What am I talking about? JaMichael, you got all types of shit going on. Like that move point in Nashville that went south. Poor, Parker, they say that Gators are still shitting out his remains."

I stood up, shocked and confused. "How do you know about, Parker?"

"JaMichael, I know about most things you don't think I know about. But that's neither here nor there." She stood up and walked to the back room. When she came back, she was wheeling a big suitcase. She kneeled down with it in the middle of the living room, laid it on its side, and opened it up. "JaMichael, you ever seen a Mach .90 before?" She pulled one of the fully automatic weapons from her bag and handed it to me.

"Hell, n'all, where did you get these from?"

"Don't worry about it. You got Grizzly and his Goons looking for you. I'm letting you know now when they find you it's going to be trouble. His niggas are heartless. That shit they did to Parker was child's play, trust and believe me on this."

I couldn't help mugging her. I needed to know how she knew so much. "What the fuck is going on, Bubbie? Tell me how you know all of this shit."

"Why does that matter? The fact is, I do know it, and since I know there are a bunch of killers looking for you and Getty it's a must that I arm you to make sure you are safe. After all, I'ma need my child's father to be around for the long haul." She lowered her head, then looked up at me all guilty like.

"Fuck is you talking about? I ain't your *child's* father." She took my hand and placed it on her stomach. "You're going to be. It's one of the reasons I was trying so hard to get into contact with you. I'm having our child, JaMichael, I'm pregnant."

I felt like the breath had been taken out of my lungs. "*Pregnant*, how could that be? We only did our thing one time. Don't it take more than that?" I was devastated.

"Apparently not baby because I'm pregnant. I'm pregnant, and I'm happy. You make me happy as long as you do the right thing. You are going to do the right thing, I'm assuming?" Her voice had a hint of a threat inside it. I peeped that immediately.

"Man, you gon' have to pee on a stick in front of me or something. Even if you are pregnant, how the fuck you know it's my baby? I know I can't be the only nigga you're sleeping with?"

She gasped, "So, what are you saying, JaMichael? You saying, you think I'm some kind of whore or something?" Now we were both up, and she was in my face looking angry.

"Man, I ain't saying you're a hoe. You know how shit goes in Memphis, everybody is doing their thing down here. You just taking shit the wrong way." I was frustrated.

I wasn't old enough to have nobody pregnant. I had shit, I had to get right in my life, and I had enemies that were apparently on my heels.

"JaMichael, you already know I don't need no man to do nothing for me. If I gotta do this shit all on my own, I'ma do just that. Trust me when I tell you." She turned her back to me and folded her arms across her chest. "So, honestly all you gotta do is tell me what you plan on doing? If you ain't fuckin' wit' me then I'm strong enough to do everything on my own."

Man, I was so fucked up in the head I didn't know what to say or do. I was imagining what life was going to be like once my seed came into the world. I didn't know if I was ready to stand up as a man and handle my responsibility. A child was a serious, long term commitment. But I also knew that coward shit wasn't in me.

"Bubbie, if the child is mine, I'm going to most definitely provide for my seed."

She was quiet for a moment, then she turned around facing me. "What do you mean if the child is yours? I'm standing here telling you, right now, I am pregnant with your baby. So, it's for you to do what you gotta do, right now. My question is what are you going to do?"

154

I was trying so hard to maintain my composure. There was a lot going on in my head that I was trying to sort out, and the more irritated she appeared, the more flustered I was becoming. "I took ahold of her shoulders and held them while I looked into her eyes. "Bubbie, listen to me, I got you. I'ma stand up and handle my bidness the way I am supposed, too. Only bitch niggas allow their woman to raise their child on their own. I might be a young nigga, but that deadbeat shit ain't in me. I got you." Even though I wasn't in the mood I kissed her lips and pulled her into my body.

She tensed at first, then she slowly but surely relented and allowed me to hug and hold her. "JaMichael, I appreciate you saying what you said, but I gotta keep shit real with you. Now that I am pregnant with your child things are about be a lot different. I gotta have that number one spot in your life. If I don't get it, she gon' get real swiftly. We need to be together for this baby, I ain't taking no for an answer." She removed herself from my embrace. "I want you all to myself. I'll clear my path if I have, too. You don't have the slightest idea who you're dealing with, but you're about to find out real soon."

Chapter 17

When I got back to the parking lot of Dee's, Phoenix was seated in the passenger's seat of Tamia's Nissan Maxima, with his arm around her. The window was cracked just a tad and I could hear him whispering a bunch of encouraging words. I stepped up to the car angrily and pulled it open. Both of them jumped and looked up at me.

Tamia had tears coming down her face. She shook her head at me, as Phoenix slid out of the car. "Lil' Momma you gon' be good. If you need anything you already know how to get up with me." He stepped beside me. "Shorty, bad Mane, you gotta treasure that diamond, or somebody else will. Believe that homeboy." He pulled his nose and smiled at her.

She smiled back weakly and wiped tears from her cheeks. "Thank you for comforting me, Phoenix. That was special."

"Don't mention it, Shorty, it's all good. Say, Potna, is my lil' cousin still upstairs?" he asked, looking me over.

I ignored his ass and slid into the passenger's seat where he was just sitting. I closed the door. "Pull off, Tamia, let me holla at you for a minute."

"JaMichael, I don't even feel like talking, right now. You've said everything you needed to say when you spun off with, Bubbie. I can get the hint."

"Man, shut yo' ass up, and pull this car out of the lot so I can holla at you. Hurry up." It was my first time really snapping on her, I could tell she was scared by how she jumped and started the engine. After we were rolling for a minute, I took a deep breath and looked over at her. There were light tears continuing to stream down her face. "Baby, first off, let me just say, I'm sorry," I started.

"Don't baby me, right now. My name is, Tamia. Until we get this all figured out you can call me, Tamia." She continued to drive. "But go ahead."

"Like I was saying, I apologize. I didn't mean to disrespect you by sliding off with her."

"Well, you did," she interrupted me.

"Man shut up and let me do this shit. I'm trying to tell yo' ass something, but every time I get started you get to cutting me off. Damn," I snapped.

She slammed on the brakes. "Get out of my car, Ja-Michael, now!" she screamed.

"What?" I looked around and saw there was about six cars behind us. We were in a section of the Orange Mound where there were gang wars jumping off. I didn't give a fuck what she was talking about I wasn't getting out of her car.

"Get out of my car, JaMichael! I can't take this shit no more. You don't give a fuck about me. All you care about is you. I'm too emotional for this shit, and you know I am!" She broke down again.

Cars were blowing their horns behind us. Tamia had stopped at a stop sign on the narrow street that led into a busy intersection. Because the street was so narrow it was nearly impossible for any car to get past our vehicle. She looked as if she didn't care about the cars trying to get us to move. All I kept thinking about was the area we were in.

"Baby, please roll-off. You and I need to talk. I know you're mad at me, but I need your ear, right now. I need you to hear me out."

She lowered her face to the steering wheel and cried harder. "Why should I, JaMichael? Why should I sit down and talk to you? You don't give a fuck about me. All I want you to do is love me. Love me, like I love you. I beg you to do this, and you can't."

"Please pull off, Baby," I said this looking over our shoulders. There were people getting out of their cars and congregating in the middle of the street. I assumed they were talking about us. I saw one dude pull out a gun and cock it. This made me take my .40 off my hip. "Tamia, drive, or we finna die."

She wiped her tears away, pulled into the intersection, made a right, and drove on. "What do you wanna say to me, JaMichael? You can start by telling me why it was so important for you to leave with, Bubbie? When you know damn well that she and I are beefing, and always have been." She sniffled.

"Baby, okay now, if you want me to tell you the truth, you're going to have to hear me out one hunnit percent."

"Long as you keep shit one hunnit percent honest with me, I'm all ears. I don't want you holding anything back either. You already know, I would never keep any secrets from you."

"The bitch put me on to some cash. I thought I was gon' wanna work for, Phoenix and Mikey goofy ass out there in Black Haven. But when that nigga Mikey started to fucking with, Jahliya, I just couldn't work under them niggas no longer. So, I was looking to do my own thing, and shorty made me a proposition that I jumped on." I tilted the passenger's seat back and exhaled.

Tamia nodded her head. "And, so is that it?"

I shook my head. "N'all, that ain't it, it turns out that she had a liking for me all along. We wound up fucking around once, and now she saying she pregnant."

Tamia blinked and tears fell out of her eyes, along with a hint of snot. She didn't even bother to wipe it away either.

"So, you mean to tell me all this time I was being faithful to you, you were going behind my back fuckin' with her? An enemy of mine!"

"You thinking way too far into it. That bitch was putting me up on cash. You ain't on shit. All that lovey-dovey shit is cool but it ain't putting no money in my pocket. In case you didn't get the memo this muthafuckin' world revolve around money. It's about the haves and have nots. I was financially losing until 'ol girl stepped in."

"You see what I'm saying, JaMichael, it's always about you. Everything you just said ain't got nothing to do with anybody else other than you. I don't know why I couldn't see this shit earlier." She wiped more tears from her face.

I squeezed her thigh and she smacked my hand away. "I'm sorry, Tamia. You know I don't give a fuck about her, I only love you. Me and you are supposed to have a future together."

Tamia kept right on driving, as she held her silence. She didn't say a word until we got to her house. She parked in their garage in the back, and we entered her home through the back door. She set her keys on the kitchen table and led me through the house.

It was dark. We took the stairs and wound up in her bedroom. She closed the door, and I sat on the bed. She started to rummage through her closet. "How could you cheat on me, JaMichael?"

"Baby, I didn't mean to. You already know she ain't got shit on you. I wasn't doing nothin' but chasing that money. You already know how I get down."

She backed out of the closet and turned around. When she did, I saw the Tech-9 in her hand. She slammed a magazine into it, cocked it and aimed the gun at me. "N'all, JaMichael, you see I thought, I knew who you were. It turns

160

out that I didn't. You don't give a fuck about me. Now you got a baby by, Bubbie. She took you away from me. My life is ruined," she cried.

I hopped off the bed and backed away. This girl was tripping. I didn't know if she had the heart to actually pull that trigger, but one thing was for sure, I didn't want to take no chances. My aunt always preached about hell having no fury like a woman scorned. "Baby, what the fuck are you doing?"

"I'm gon' kill you, JaMichael, then I'm gon' kill myself. I'm not about to let that bitch ruin my life. I'll be damned if I allow that after all, we've been through." Her finger wavered on the trigger.

I was wondering if I could up my gun fast enough before she pulled her trigger. But then again if I upped it, I didn't know if I was prepared to smoke Tamia. I cared about her a lot. I needed to find a way to diffuse the situation. I knew she was emotional, so I decided to play into that.

"Look, Tamia, I'm sorry baby. I'm so so sorry for hurting you. You have no idea how much I love you, Tamia. I fucked up baby, and I probably deserve to die for betraying you. But if I'm dead how will I ever get a chance to prove my love to you? How will I ever get the chance to make you my wife one of these days?"

She shook her head slightly. "You would never marry me, JaMichael. Don't say that."

I took a chance, I slowly lowered myself to one knee. I was trying to do anything to stop her from pulling that trigger. "Baby, ain't nobody other than you going to be my wife. All I see is you, all I need is you, baby. You are my whole entire universe. I don't care what you say, you're going to be my wife. It's us, Boo."

Tamia started to shake, before she lowered the gun, and hung her head. She started crying harder than I had ever witnessed before.

She walked over to me and laid the gun on her bed. "I love you so much, JaMichael. Why are you hurting me like this? You're supposed to be the one that protects me. Instead, all you're doing is tearing me down. I can't take this pain that you are rendering onto me." She balled my shirt into her fists and cried into my shoulder.

I felt horrible, I felt sick, I felt low, and I wished I had never inflicted that pain on to her. "I'm sorry, Boo, please forgive me. You already know how much Daddy loves you."

When I said this, she shivered. She hugged me and sighed against my neck. "I think I know the real reason you started to fuck with that bitch, JaMichael," she whispered.

"Baby, I already told you why."

She took a step back and pulled her blouse over her head. "N'all, it's deeper than that. There is only one way for a woman to fully conquer her man, and it starts right between my thighs. My mother always told me that." She pulled her skirt down, and tossed it aside, then stepped out of her panties. Her garden looked extra chunky this night. "If this is what it's going to take for me to lock you down, I might as well give you some of what you been craving." Her fingers played through her trimmed lips. She slightly opened herself and flashed me her pink insides.

I got hard as a rock, I knew she was vulnerable and the right thing to do would have been to set my list aside to cater to her emotionally, but I wanted to fuck Tamia so bad. I wanted to see what that pussy felt like. However, I still had to play my role. "Baby, I'ma love you whether we do something or not. I got my whole life to be with you. The last thing I wanna do is rush you into anything."

She kissed my lips and slid my hand in between her thighs. "You ain't rushing me to do nothin' I don't want to do. The only thing that pisses me off is that Bubbie was able to get some of my man before I was. That irks my soul." She kissed me again. "JaMichael, I want you to be my first," with that being said she started to unfastened my Gucci belt. "Do you think you can do that?"

Chapter 18

Tamia laid on her stomach, with her face laying on a fluffy pillow. I kissed along her shoulder blades. Then kissed down her spine. She moaned while I rubbed her juicy booty. I spread the cheeks, sought out her pussy lips and slid my middle finger into her heat. It felt like a wet furnace.

She looked over her shoulder and moaned loudly. "Un-nhh, Daddy, that feels good."

I got behind her, leaned down, stuck my face between her thighs, and kissed her coochie. She spread her thighs further apart, now I was really able to get into there, so I could do my thing.

"Daddy-Daddy-Daddy—ooo, that feel so good!" She got on all fours, and I started eating her from the back, hungrily while she held the headboard, and moaned louder and louder.

I couldn't help stroking my piece. I was so geeked to finally get me some of Tamia. Her body had been calling me ever since we were kids. She rested her face on the bed and pulled her cheeks open for me. I was so thirsty that I licked up and down her crevice, sucked on her lips, and pulled on them. Then my tongue was in her back door sliding in and out.

"Uh-uh-uh, Daddy, oh shit!" she moaned. Her fingers went between her thighs and wound up in her slit. She pinched her clit while I licked her fingers. She tasted so good. "I want you to do me, Daddy. Please-I'm ready—please!" She fell on her stomach.

I pushed her right thigh to her rib cage and continued to attack that cat with my tongue and lips. It was oozing by this point and dripping down her caramel thighs.

"You want Daddy huh, Baby?" I worked two fingers inside of her and pulled them out, sucking them into my mouth. Then my tongue was going back and forth across her clit until she screamed and came all over my fingers. I pushed her on her back, and forced her knees to her chest, eating away until she came some more.

By the time I laid back, and she worked her face into my lap, she was so horny her fingers were gliding in and out of her sex lips. "I'm ready-I'm ready, Daddy—please!" She wrapped my piece into her little hand and pumped me as fast as she could. Then she was sucking on my head loudly, licking around it with her tongue. "Please Daddy, my kitty is ready."

"Okay, baby, come on then." I guided her backward, got between her thick thighs, took my dick, and ran it up and down her slit. It felt hot, I could feel the heat beating off it.

"Come on, Daddy. I want you to love me. As soon as you get some of me, you can love me for real. I just know you will," she said opening her thighs wide.

I grabbed her little hand and placed it on my manhood. "Are you sure you're ready, Baby? Tell me that you are."

In response, she took hold of him and slid it partway into her box. "Unnhhh, Daddy, it hurt a little." She tried to ease more inside but lost her nerve. Her juices fizzed around me, and slid down onto my balls, dripping off them.

I felt like I was too close to turn back. I'd been chasing that cat for a long time, and I wasn't about to abort the mission. I grabbed her by the thighs and pulled her to me. Took myself and lined it up, before slamming it home like a savage.

"Unnhhhh, fuck!"

Her right thigh was tossed on my shoulder, then I was fucking her hard. Breaking through the barrier that was supposed to prevent me from turning her into a woman. She felt hot and incredibly tight. As soon as I was in, I long stroked her, sucking on her neck.

"Daddy-aw, shit! Uh-uh, Daddy, I can't! Ooo-ooo, shit!" she screamed.

Then she was cumming, shaking as if she was having a seizure. I kept right on pumping, her pussy felt like a fist. It squeezed me more and more. She was so wet, I could hear the sounds of our lovemaking. That excited me all the more. I pushed her pretty titties together and sucked on the elongated nipples. Then pulled them with my teeth and sent my tongue in circles around them. Her breasts felt firm and supple. The harder I sucked on them it seems the wetter her box got until she was cumming again.

I waited until she came down, then I flipped on my back and guided her on top of me. She eased back on to my dick and tried her best to ride me slow with her little titties bouncing up and down.

She kept her mouth wide open. Breathing heavy. "Come on, Boo, work these lil' hips for me." Rotate them in a circle.

"Unhhh-unhhh, Daddy, okay—okay!" She placed her hands on my chest and went to work. Her kitty continued to ooze worse than ever. The feeling kept on getting better and better for me. "Like this, Daddy—uh-shit-like this?"

I grabbed that fat ass booty and helped her pick up some speed. "Yeah, Boo."

Then she started bouncing up and down on me like a bouncy house. Milking me, for all I was worth. I could literally feel the scales inside of her pussy. When I saw a line of drool seep out of the corner of her mouth, I started cumming pumping up into her hard while she slammed down into my lap. Then she was cumming again, collapsing onto me, shaking like crazy.

****

We'd been laying in her bed tangle up within each other when she licked my neck and grabbed my piece in her small hand. "JaMichael, are you serious that one day you're going to marry me?"

I had my eyes closed because I was tired as hell. The room smelled like straight sex. I was too tired to even get up and get in her shower. "Yeah, Boo, I'm serious. I mean we're still kids, right now, but when we get older and get things more established, then yes. You are going to be my wife."

She hugged me tighter. "That makes me so happy to hear you say that. I've been in love with you ever since I was a little girl. I always knew you would be the one to take my virginity. And I always knew one day you would be my husband. You mean the world to me. Even though, I hate you for getting, Bubbie pregnant. Ain't you gon' make that bitch have an abortion?"

I gripped her left ass cheek and squeezed it. There was nothing like having a thick ass female laid all over you the way that she was on me. I knew I loved her, and I was down to say whatever I needed to in order to keep her happy at that point. "Baby, I don't even know if the kid is mine. I ain't the only nigga she was fucking."

Tamia was silent, she straddled me and looked down into my face. The moonlight shined through the open window of her bedroom. "That's not answering my question. I need to know you are not even going to let things get that

168

far. You need to kill that project before it even has time to manifest itself inside of her womb. If you want a kid, I'll give you a kid. After all, I love you. That bitch, Bubbie, don't know the first thing about loving you."

"Baby, I'll do anything for you, but I don't know about killing no kids. I ain't never been down with some shit like that. If the child turns out to be mine, I ain't got no other choice other than to stand up and be a man. It's already too many bitch niggas out here neglecting their children. I ain't gon' be one of them."

Tamia climbed off me. As soon as she got up, I felt cold as hell. I could smell her pussy as clear as day. "This is some bullshit, JaMichael. How can you say you love me, then you'll turn around and have a family with another woman? Not only that, but it's a female who I've had bad blood with ever since I was a kid. There is nothing you can possibly say that will make this all better. What it all comes down to, is that you betrayed me in the worst way possible."

I felt devastated because she had a point. I got up and stood before her naked, then tried to pull her to me. "Baby, come here."

She jerked away from me. "N'all, JaMichael, it ain't about to be that easy. I know, I'm all vulnerable regarding you and all of that, but I'm not an idiot. You played me like a fool."

Once again, I tried to hold her, but she backed away from me and even had the audacity to swipe at my hands. "Get away from me, Baby. I ain't feeling you, right now." She turned her back to me. "Nigga you don't even know, I would die for your ass. I'm not even an adult, but I will seriously give up my life for you." She fell to her knees and busted out crying. "And now you're about to have a baby with this bitch. Where the fuck does that leave me, Ja-Michael?"

I was sick on the stomach. I kneeled down and shuffled across the carpet until I had my arm around her. Then our cheeks were resting against each other. I loved Tamia. Always had, I think ever since I was a shorty. Just like Jahliya, I hated when she cried, or was in any sort of pain, especially if it was inflicted by me.

"Baby, please just tell me what I can do to make things all better. I never meant to hurt you. Just tell me what you need, please?"

She shook her head and cried harder. She wrapped her arms around her body and began to rock. "She's trying to ruin us, JaMichael, and you let her. You're allowing her to break us apart, and it's not fair. You're supposed to protect me. I'm supposed to be your, baby. You're not supposed to let anybody hurt me if you can help it." She sniffled and the waterworks became more intense.

Damn, I was feeling like shit. "What do you want me to do, Tamia? I'll do anything for you."

"Make sure she don't have that kid. Convince her to get the situation taken care of. I'll give you your first seed. That's what I'm supposed to do anyway because I am going to be your wife one day. Can you do that?"

I was willing to agree to whatever she needed to hear. I wasn't about to tell her, I didn't believe in abortions. Or that no matter how much I loved her, I would never allow Bubbie to kill my seed. I didn't know how we were going to work through this, but I knew we were going to make it. We loved each other.

"Baby, me and her are going to have a long talk. You got my word, we are going to figure this shit out. I don't like to seeing you hurting the way that you are. I sincerely apologize." I wrapped her into my arms again.

"Thank you, JaMichael. Thank you for going the extra mile to get things figured out with her and thank you for apologizing. That really means the world to me." She kissed my cheek and allowed me to pick her up and carry her to the bed. I accidentally placed her on top of the Tech, she hollered out in pain and moved it from under her.

I placed it on the floor. We snuggled up, with me be-hind her. As soon as we were in place we were out like a light.

Chapter 19

Two weeks later as I was coming from Costco with Veronica, Getty slammed on his brakes in front of the house and jumped out of his car. Leaving the door open, he ran around it, and up to me. "JaMichael—JaMichael! Them niggas kilt my mother man. They killed my 'ol girl." He fell to his knees, with tears pouring down his face.

Veronica looked stunned. She grabbed the last bit of grocery bags and hurried up the porch steps. She stopped when she got to the top of them. "JaMichael, before you go anywhere you make sure you come in and let me know. Don't go out there doing nothing crazy. Do you hear me?"

"Yes, ma'am."

Veronica gave Getty a look of sympathy before she disappeared into the house.

Then I was kneeled beside him, with my arm around his shoulder. "Who took your 'ol girl, Getty?"

He shook his head from left to right. "That fuck nigga, Grizzly. He left me a note in her blood. I ain't about to take this shit lying down. I'm finna go at this nigga. I found out where some of his Potnas are laying their heads. I wanna get at them, niggas. They are for sure to lead me right to him. What do you say, are you fucking wit' me?"

I stood up, then helped him come to his feet. "Nigga you know that. What I look like allowing you to avenge your mother's death on your own?" I hugged him.

He held me longer than I expected. "This shit ain't right, JaMichael. We play in these streets just like the next nigga but we ain't never went at a mafucka's Mama. But that's how these niggas are playin' the game now. So, okay, fair exchange ain't no robbery." He wiped his face.

"When are you trying to move on them, niggas?" I asked hoping I had a few days.

Me and Jahliya were moving out of Veronica's crib in two days. I was excited for us to be moving into our own spot. Bubbie was begging me to come and stay with her even though that was the last thing on my mind. I had yet to ask her what she had in mind for our dealings together. Me and Getty had been hustling like me crazy, and it was almost time for us to re-up from Bubbie again. That was going to be hard to do because I'd been ignoring her for nearly a week, and she hated when I did that shit. I was too busy going into overdrive for Tamia. I was doing all I could to emotionally restore her because it was important to me to do just that.

"We can move on them niggas this weekend. I got a lil more digging to do. I need to make sure, I know what I know, you feel me?" The sun came from behind the clouds and caused the block to light up.

It was eleven in the morning, and already I could tell it was going to be a hot day.

I hugged the homie again. "Look, you do whatever you need to do. I'm riding with you, a'ight."

"Say less, my nigga, that's all I needed to here." He broke our embrace and jogged back to his car. Before getting in he looked over at me. "JaMichael, everybody needs a real friend that's going through the type of shit I am. I love you, homie. That's on my soul I do, Joe." He got inside his car and drove off.

I shook my head. I stopped to think about my own mother being murdered. I was too little to understand what had taken place with her situation, but over the years I had gotten a variety of different stories. I didn't know what to believe, all I knew was that she was gone, and I felt like I needed her every day that she was.

As I was making my way back into the house Jahliya pulled up in a fire red Porsche truck and stepped out of the vehicle. She was dressed in a Christian Dior body-hugging skirt dress that complimented her frame. My jealousy of imagining what another nigga thought when he was able to see her looking all good like that kicked in. My face was screwed up. I tried my best to fix it before she was able to tell the difference.

"Baby, brother, where the hell you been all night?" she asked, grabbing her Birken bag from the passenger's seat. Then she was walking up to me. I saw how the skirt dress stopped mid-thigh. Both of her caramel thighs were on display. It looked as if she'd put on a little weight.

"I stayed out with, Tamia. Her moms had to work a double, and she ain't wanna be alone. You know how that shit go." I hugged her after she walked into my open arms. She smelled good, as usual.

"Yeah, well, once again I was hitting yo' ass up all night worried. Why you ain't return none of my calls, or texts?"

Come to think about it, I hadn't received any calls or texts since last night after I got to Tamia's house. I grabbed my phone, and played with it for a second, before discovering it was on do not disturb. "Damn sis, I musta put this on do not disturb or something."

"N'all, Tamia musta put it on that feature, but it's all good." She kissed me on the lips and wrapped her arm around my lower waist. "Come on, I need to shower, and then I want you to hold me. Auntie supposed to be going to work in a minute. When she do, I wanna show you something." She dragged her hand down the material of her skirt, and stopped at her upper thighs, looking into my eyes the whole time.

Before I could respond, Veronica stepped out on the porch, with a phone in her hand. "Kids, Taurus is on the phone. He wanna talk to y'all."

I felt Jahliya freeze under me, then a slight chill went down my back. I hadn't even heard my father's name out of anybody's mouth in a while. I pulled Jahliya closer to me possessive like and tried to get her to calm down. "Auntie, what did you say."

"Your Father is calling from Terra Haute, Indiana. He wants to talk with both of you. Y'all better hurry up. Their phone calls are only but so long," she reminded.

"A'ight, here we come." I waited until Veronica went back in the house with the phone, then I turned Jahliya around so she could face me. "You okay, baby girl?"

She took a deep breath and nodded her head. "Yeah, I'm good. I don't know if I'm ready to talk to him, Ja-Michael. He killed our mothers. What type of man would kill his baby mothers?"

"We don't know if he killed her or not. The family is also saying that Grandma Deborah coulda done it. We just don't know." I kissed her cheek and hugged her. "But come on in here so we can see what he wants."

Jahliya broke out of my embrace and raced back to her truck. "I ain't ready to talk to him yet, JaMichael. I just ain't." She jumped in the truck and stormed away from the curb.

****

When I got into the house Veronica was still talking on the phone. She saw me and handed it over to me. "Your daddy wanna talk to you, JaMichael. He got about fifteen minutes left." She kissed me on the cheek and rubbed my back before leaving out of the living room. "Good luck."

I took the phone and sat down on the couch. Then took a deep breath before placing it to my hear. I didn't know what I was going to say, or how I felt about talking to the man that may have been responsible for killing my mother, Blaze.

After stalling for a full minute, I placed the phone to my ear. "Hello?"

"Son, how are you?"

"I'm a'ight. What's good wit' you doe, Pops?"

"I'm alive for the time being, and that's all that matters to me. How is, Jahliya?"

"She good, she just ain't ready to talk to you yet. She got a few things going on, you know how life is."

"I do." He was quiet for a brief moment. "Listen, son, I want you to come and see me. You and your sister, but if she's not ready to come, I ain't gon' sweat it. Although I would love to see her as well."

"Pop, you're all the way in Indiana. How we supposed to get down there?" I asked kicking off my Jordan's. Veronica really didn't like for us to be wearing shoes in the house, and I planned on having me and Jahliya's pad the same way.

"I'm sending for y'all son. I'll make sure all the expenses are paid. All you and she would have to do is get into the limo, I'll be sending. Then my mans gon' scoop y'all up in a Chopper. You'll be put up in a topnotch hotel, and treated like royalty, you got my word on that."

I nodded, everything sounded good. Plus, there was a major part of me that wanted to finally meet my father in person. I was tired of hearing about the legend of Taurus without actually been given the chance to meet him in person. After all, I had so many questions. There were so many things, I wanted to know about him. So, many empty spaces I needed to be filled inside my heart and soul.

"Pop, before I agree to anything. I need to know if you really killed my mother, and if so, what would make you do that to her?"

"Damn, Ghost, we ain't got time to get into all that over this phone. We got about five minutes before the call is over, but I will say this son, I would never hurt Blaze, or should I say your mother. I loved her with all my heart. I don't think I would never love another woman like I did both you and Jahliya's mother. But to answer your question, no."

"That's all I needed to hear, I'll be there. I can't speak on my older sister, but I will most definitely be there," I assured him, just as Veronica came, and stood in the doorway dressed in a short red robe that did a poor job of concealing her thighs.

"Okay, let me get everything in order, we'll go from there. Give the phone back to, Veronica. I got like two minutes left until I gotta go, but I will be calling again soon. I love you, son! Make sure you tell my Princess, I love her as well."

"I love you too, Pops." I handed the phone back to Veronica, and she stepped out of the room with it still placed to her ear. I got up and went into my bedroom. My mind was thrown off, I couldn't help thinking about my father and meeting him for the first time.

Danyelle came into the bedroom and closed the door behind her. She stood with her back to it and had a mischievous look in her eyes. She had on a yellow Fendi sundress that stopped mid-thigh. Her toes were bare, and the nails were freshly done. She locked the door and slowly walked over to me until she was standing directly in front of me.

She took ahold of my hands and placed them on her hips. "Why you don't even pay attention to me, JaMichael? Every time I come over here you don't give me the time of day. You rather fuck with my mother than to mess with me." She made my hands roam and lift her dress just enough to flash the sight of her pink lace front shorts that were all up in her monkey. I could see the mold of her mound as clear as day.

I pulled my hand back. "Shorty, if you don't get yo' ass out of here, I'ma tell yo' mama on you."

She shrugged her shoulders. "I don't care. What she gon' do, try and tell me not to do some shit that she is doing?" She straddled my lap and held onto my big shoulders.

Now I coulda easily pushed her off me, but for some reason, I just wanted to see how far she was going to go. "Oh, so you think you grown now?"

She nodded. "Yep, you fucking around with Jahliya, and my mama. I done heard you with both of them. I got the same things they got, but mine is fresher. Yet, you don't give me the time of day. Well, my mama here, right now, so we can't do nothin', but I'm just letting you know, I want you to try this out, too." She took my right hand and slid it under her dress, pulling her panties to the side.

Her pussy was hairless and felt hot. That freaky shit was in me. I ran my finger up and down her slit and even dared to dip him inside of her all the way to the second knuckle.

She licked my earlobe. "Mmm, that's what I'm talking about cuz. What's good for the goose is good for the gander." She came face to face and we wound up tonguing each other down, while my finger went in and out of her pussy. In a matter of seconds, she was sopping wet.

My dick was hard as a baseball bat. She scooted back, and kneeled down, pulling him out of my shorts, stroking him up and down. She was just about to put him into her mouth when Veronica knocked once and opened the door to the bedroom.

"Ghost I—" When she saw what her daughter was doing her eyes got bucked. She dropped the cellphone we had been talking to Taurus on and froze.

I jumped up with my piece throbbing like crazy. Danyelle stood up and pulled her dress down. Her nipples were sticking up against the material. "Mama, we was just playing around. Please don't overreact," she said right away.

Veronica acted as if she was speechless. She simply mugged Danyelle, then eyed me with extreme anger. "How long has this been going on, Ghost?"

"This the first time, Auntie, and we really wasn't on nothin'. We were just playing around," I assured her.

Danyelle smacked her lips. "Mama, I don't mean no disrespect, but I know you ain't finna act all high and mighty. I caught you two doing your own thing before. I didn't make a big deal out of it. He's the only male here, and we're all family, so it's like who cared. We were only playing around, there is no harm in that."

Veronica frowned, then laughed angrily. "Lil' girl, first of all, I'm grown. You're a child, and you stay under my roof. Secondly, that is your family, y'all ain't supposed to be doing none of that. Lastly, you don't worry about what the fuck I do because I am the adult. I do whatever I wanna do. You understand me?"

Danyelle's pursed her lips and crossed her arms in front of her looking off toward the ceiling. "Yes, ma'am. Is there anything else?"

Veronica was quiet. She kept mugging Danyelle as if she was trying to find something to say, finally, she pointed toward the hallway. "Just go, Danyelle, I'll be in there to talk with you in a minute. First, I need to holla at your cousin Ghost because he knows better."

"But it wasn't his fault it was mine. So, if you're mad at anybody it's me. I came on to him, shoot, he fine," Danyelle added, looking into my eyes.

Veronica pointed again. Danyelle eased her way out of the room. She turned around to look me over one last time before heading into the hallway. Veronica closed the door in her face.

She waited for a second, then she turned around slowly until she was looking me over. "What's up with you, Ghost. Danyelle—really?"

"What's wrong with me!" Danyelle yelled.

"Lil' girl take yo' ass in that room and wait for me. Now!"

I don't know if Danyelle left or not, but I didn't hear anything else from her. "Auntie, I was tripping. But you already know how fine her lil' ass is with them pretty eyes, and all that. This was her first time coming at me, and before I could think things through she was getting ready to buss me down."

Veronica stepped into my face and shook her head. "Boy, you already know I'm going through a custody battle over her. The last thing I need right now is for any of this to get back to her father."

"Well, it's a good thing you came when you did." I stepped into her face. "So, what you gon' do? You gon' whoop me or something?" Every time I stepped forward; she took a step back. It wound up with her back against the door like her daughter's back just was.

"Boy if you don't back yo' ass up we gon' have a problem," she threatened.

That threat was hollow to me. I got into her face and placed my forehead against hers. Then with blazing speed, I cuffed that ass. "I ain't trying to fuck with her anyway, she just a lil' girl," I said low enough for only her to hear me. "I want some of this grown shit, right here." I leaned her back, and sucked her neck, sliding my hands under her shirt. Once they were under there, I got to tweaking them nipples. It didn't take long before they were as hard as Danyelle's were. I pulled her blouse all the way up and took to sucking one into my mouth at a time.

She tried her best to break away from me but wasn't nothing mobbing. Danyelle had me riled up, and the fact that Veronica had caught up only made the shit that much more exciting to me. I didn't understand why I was like I was, but I craved some of Veronica. She was so strapped it was crazy.

I slammed her back against the wall and sucked her neck. She started to moan and push at the same time. "Stop, Ghost! Stop, before Danyelle hears us," she hissed giving me a forceful push.

I stumbled backward, just as I heard Jahliya's car pulling up to the curb in front of the house. I could tell it was her because she was banging that *Dej Loaf*. She was always banging her for some reason. Veronica broke away from me and fixed her clothes before running her fingers through her hair.

"Damn you, JaMichael. You gon' get me in trouble one of these days. I can only say no for so long before you get me. You so damn fine too, JaMichael. I hate end admitting that."

I turned her around and pushed her face first into the wall. Then I sucked all over the back of her neck and grounded into her ass. "Sooner or later I'ma get this pussy, Auntie. I ain't forget what you used to do to me when I was little. All that shit is still very vivid in my head." I slipped my hand around, into her panties and slid two fingers inside of her box right away. Her pussy felt just as tight as Danyelle's. That made me crazy hard.

Jahliya slammed the front door and came into the house. I could hear her calling out for me. I yanked my hand out of Veronica's panties, and rushed into our bathroom, and closed the door.

Two minutes later, Jahliya was knocking on it. "Ja-Michael, open the door. I need to talk to you lil' brother."

Chapter 20

I still couldn't believe my eyes. Jahliya had dumped ten bricks of the Rebirth on our bed. They were wrapped in yellow aluminum foiled packages. She held one of them in her hand.

"JaMichael, we gotta get the fuck out of Memphis. When that nigga, Mikey find out I hit him this hard, he's for sure to come looking for me." She sat on the bed.

I still couldn't believe she had ten bricks of the Rebirth. The Rebirth was strong heroin that when used it made the hypes feel like they were high for the first time every time. Not only that, it was highly addictive. So addictive that a person would be ready to give up their lives than go a day without having the Rebirth in their system. Those ten bricks were valued at five million dollars easily if we were to beak them down and sell them on the streets bag by bag, instead of moving weight. I was prepared to do whatever we had to do to change our lives. Plus, I also wanted to start writing my books and movies. I had big dreams that offing those bricks could help bring into fruition.

"Jahliya, if we leave Memphis, where the fuck is, we going to go?" I asked, still appraising the money we could make off the work.

"I don't know, but we can't stay here. Maybe we could go to Atlanta, or over to our family in Chicago. I don't care where we go, but wherever we go we gotta go fast." She took the bricks and started putting them into a duffle bag.

"How long you think it's gon take before he know that this shit is gone?"

She shrugged her shoulders. "Lil' bruh that nigga took me to a warehouse full of this shit. They fuckin' with some white girl named, Nastia. Supposedly she used to fuck with our father, Taurus. I don't know how everything lines up, but this chick is loaded. To be honest with you I don't even think he'll know, it's gone for at least a week. He's trying to put on so many cats, and they are grinding hard for him hollering that Duffle Bag Cartel shit. Nastia, is a major plug and she's from Russia." She zipped the bag and took it to the closet.

"If she's from Russia how in the hell do she know our father?" I asked watching her stuff the bag into the back of the closet and close the sliding doors.

Jahliya shrugged again. "Apparently dad was all over the world fuckin' some of every kind of broad. I don't know how much he was tied into her, but she's having major money now. I mean, I don't know how much she was having back then, but I can tell you, right now, she is loaded." Jahliya came and sat on the bed. "So, what you think we should do?"

I sat beside her and allowed her to lay her head on my shoulder. "On some real shit, I don't care where we are just as long as you are beside me, I just wanna make you happy. Straight up."

"Awww uh, you always gotta make me all sappy and shit. Don't you know, it's a time and a place for all of that shit?" she teased, kissing my cheek.

I smiled. "I'm just saying what's on my heart, that's all. You know, you're my world big sis."

Jahliya stood up and got undressed. She kept on her bra and panties and slid under the covers. "I'm tired as hell. Mikey had me up all night trying to show me how he runs his operation. I don't know why he feels the need to jack to me, but whatever. I wound up coming up with five million dollars worth of product. That's major." She yawned and covered her mouth with her fist.

Because she yawned, I wound up doing the same thing. I was all of a sudden tired. I wanted to just curl up behind her, and spoon.

She pulled back the covers and patted the bed. "Get yo' swoll ass in here with me and wrap those arms around me boy." I could see the thong going up the crack of her ass. It looked like she'd put on some weight over the past few weeks.

I threw my shirt off and slid behind her. She backed all the way up and pulled the covers over us. My face rested in the back of her head. "You honestly ready to leave all of this shit in Memphis behind?" I asked kissing her scalp.

"Yeah, I don't think that there is anything else for us here. I mean you're finishing school, and I don't have anything going here. I think it'll be in our best interest to start somewhere new. Memphis is washed up, has been for a long time."

I held her firmer. "You know Pops saying he wanna see you when I go down there."

"Aw, so you did wind up talking to him, huh? Did you ask him if he killed our mothers?" she asked dryly.

"You already know I did, and he basically told me, he would never hurt either one of them. But I'm sure he'll explain more once we go to see him."

"What do you mean we? I ain't never said I was going to see that man. I still don't feel like I'm ready. I just think that—"

She was cut off by the sounds of a large banging coming from the back of the house. Then cars slammed on their brakes in front of the house. I could hear multiple car doors open up. I jumped out of the bed and grabbed my .40 caliber from off the dresser and rushed to the window. When I looked out of it, I saw Mikey coming up the steps with two guns in his hand and a mug on his face. There were five masked men behind him. He walked right up to the door and kicked it as hard as he could.

"You punk ass bitch! Open up this muthafuckin' door and take what you got coming to you!"

Before I could even think about what I was doing, I was aiming the .40 out of the window, and placing my finger on the trigger. Wasn't nobody about to hurt my sister. I didn't give a fuck who Mikey was. "Jahliya get down!" I pulled the trigger.

To Be Continued...
Heartless Goon 2
Coming Soon

Submission Guideline

Submit the first three chapters of your completed manuscript to ldpsubmissions@gmail.com, subject line: Your book's title. The manuscript must be in a .doc file and sent as an attachment. Document should be in Times New Roman, double spaced and in size 12 font. Also, provide your synopsis and full contact information. If sending multiple submissions, they must each be in a separate email.

Have a story but no way to send it electronically? You can still submit to LDP/Ca$h Presents. Send in the first three chapters, written or typed, of your completed manuscript to:

LDP: Submissions Dept
Po Box 870494
Mesquite, Tx 75187

DO NOT send original manuscript. Must be a duplicate.

Provide your synopsis and a cover letter containing your full contact information.

Thanks for considering LDP and Ca$h Presents.

<u>Coming Soon from Lock Down Publications/Ca$h Presents</u>

BOW DOWN TO MY GANGSTA

By **Ca$h**

TORN BETWEEN TWO

By **Coffee**

BLOOD STAINS OF A SHOTTA **III**

By **Jamaica**

STEADY MOBBIN **III**

By **Marcellus Allen**

RENEGADE BOYS IV

By Meesha

BLOOD OF A BOSS **VI**

SHADOWS OF THE GAME II

By **Askari**

LOYAL TO THE GAME **IV**

LIFE OF SIN **III**

By **T.J. & Jelissa**

A DOPEBOY'S PRAYER **II**

By **Eddie "Wolf" Lee**

IF LOVING YOU IS WRONG... **III**

By **Jelissa**

TRUE SAVAGE **VII**

By **Chris Green**

BLAST FOR ME **III**

DUFFLE BAG CARTEL **IV**

HEARTLESS GOON **II**

By **Ghost**

ADDICTIED TO THE DRAMA **III**

By **Jamila Mathis**

A HUSTLER'S DECEIT III

KILL ZONE **II**

BAE BELONGS TO ME III

SOUL OF A MONSTER II

By **Aryanna**

THE COST OF LOYALTY **III**

By **Kweli**

A GANGSTER'S SYN II

By **J-Blunt**

KING OF NEW YORK V

RISE TO POWER III

COKE KINGS III

By **T.J. Edwards**

GORILLAZ IN THE BAY IV

De'Kari

THE STREETS ARE CALLING II

Duquie Wilson

KINGPIN KILLAZ IV

STREET KINGS III

PAID IN BLOOD II

Hood Rich

SINS OF A HUSTLA II

ASAD

TRIGGADALE III

Elijah R. Freeman

MARRIED TO A BOSS III

By Destiny Skai & Chris Green

KINGZ OF THE GAME IV

Playa Ray

SLAUGHTER GANG III

RUTHLESS HEART

By Willie Slaughter

THE HEART OF A SAVAGE II

By Jibril Williams

FUK SHYT II

By Blakk Diamond

THE DOPEMAN'S BODYGAURD II

By Tranay Adams

TRAP GOD

By Troublesome

YAYO

By S. Allen

GHOST MOB

Stilloan Robinson

KINGPIN DREAMS

By Paper Boi Rari

CREAM

By Yolanda Moore

<u>Available Now</u>
<u>RESTRAINING ORDER</u> **I & II**
By **CA$H & Coffee**
<u>LOVE KNOWS NO BOUNDARIES</u> **I II & III**
By **Coffee**
<u>RAISED AS A GOON I, II, III & IV</u>
<u>BRED BY THE SLUMS I, II, III</u>
<u>BLAST FOR ME I & II</u>
<u>ROTTEN TO THE CORE I II III</u>
<u>A BRONX TALE I, II, III</u>
<u>DUFFEL BAG CARTEL I II III</u>
<u>HEARTLESS GOON</u>
<u>A SAVAGE DOPEBOY</u>
<u>HEARTLESS GOON</u>
By **Ghost**
<u>LAY IT DOWN</u> **I & II**
<u>LAST OF A DYING BREED</u>
<u>BLOOD STAINS OF A SHOTTA I & II</u>
By **Jamaica**
<u>LOYAL TO THE GAME</u>
<u>LOYAL TO THE GAME II</u>
<u>LOYAL TO THE GAME III</u>
<u>LIFE OF SIN I, II</u>
By **TJ & Jelissa**
<u>BLOODY COMMAS I & II</u>
<u>SKI MASK CARTEL I II & III</u>

Ghost

KING OF NEW YORK I II,III IV

RISE TO POWER I II

COKE KINGS I II

BORN HEARTLESS

By **T.J. Edwards**

IF LOVING HIM IS WRONG…I & II

LOVE ME EVEN WHEN IT HURTS I II III

By **Jelissa**

WHEN THE STREETS CLAP BACK I & II III

By **Jibril Williams**

A DISTINGUISHED THUG STOLE MY HEART I II & III

LOVE SHOULDN'T HURT I II III IV

RENEGADE BOYS I II III

By **Meesha**

A GANGSTER'S CODE I &, II III

A GANGSTER'S SYN

By **J-Blunt**

PUSH IT TO THE LIMIT

By **Bre' Hayes**

BLOOD OF A BOSS **I, II, III, IV, V**

SHADOWS OF THE GAME

By **Askari**

THE STREETS BLEED MURDER **I, II & III**

THE HEART OF A GANGSTA I II& III

By **Jerry Jackson**

CUM FOR ME

CUM FOR ME 2

194

CUM FOR ME 3

CUM FOR ME 4

CUM FOR ME 5

An **LDP Erotica Collaboration**

BRIDE OF A HUSTLA **I II & II**

THE FETTI GIRLS **I, II& III**

CORRUPTED BY A GANGSTA I, II III, IV

BLINDED BY HIS LOVE

By **Destiny Skai**

WHEN A GOOD GIRL GOES BAD

By **Adrienne**

THE COST OF LOYALTY I II

By Kweli

A GANGSTER'S REVENGE **I II III & IV**

THE BOSS MAN'S DAUGHTERS

THE BOSS MAN'S DAUGHTERS II

THE BOSSMAN'S DAUGHTERS III

THE BOSSMAN'S DAUGHTERS IV

THE BOSS MAN'S DAUGHTERS **V**

A SAVAGE LOVE **I & II**

BAE BELONGS TO ME I II

A HUSTLER'S DECEIT I, II, III

WHAT BAD BITCHES DO I, II, III

SOUL OF A MONSTER

KILL ZONE

By **Aryanna**

A KINGPIN'S AMBITON

A KINGPIN'S AMBITION **II**

I MURDER FOR THE DOUGH

By **Ambitious**

TRUE SAVAGE

TRUE SAVAGE II

TRUE SAVAGE **III**

TRUE SAVAGE **IV**

TRUE SAVAGE **V**

TRUE SAVAGE **VI**

By **Chris Green**

A DOPEBOY'S PRAYER

By **Eddie "Wolf" Lee**

THE KING CARTEL **I, II & III**

By **Frank Gresham**

THESE NIGGAS AIN'T LOYAL **I, II & III**

By **Nikki Tee**

GANGSTA SHYT **I II &III**

By **CATO**

THE ULTIMATE BETRAYAL

By **Phoenix**

BOSS'N UP **I , II & III**

By **Royal Nicole**

I LOVE YOU TO DEATH

By Destiny J

I RIDE FOR MY HITTA

I STILL RIDE FOR MY HITTA

By **Misty Holt**

LOVE & CHASIN' PAPER

By **Qay Crockett**

TO DIE IN VAIN

SINS OF A HUSTLA

By **ASAD**

BROOKLYN HUSTLAZ

By **Boogsy Morina**

BROOKLYN ON LOCK I & II

By **Sonovia**

GANGSTA CITY

By **Teddy Duke**

A DRUG KING AND HIS DIAMOND I & II III

A DOPEMAN'S RICHES

HER MAN, MINE'S TOO I, II

CASH MONEY HO'S

By Nicole Goosby

TRAPHOUSE KING **I II & III**

KINGPIN KILLAZ I II III

STREET KINGS I II

PAID IN BLOOD

By **Hood Rich**

LIPSTICK KILLAH **I, II, III**

CRIME OF PASSION I & II

By **Mimi**

STEADY MOBBN' **I, II, III**

By **Marcellus Allen**

WHO SHOT YA **I, II, III**

Renta

GORILLAZ IN THE BAY **I II III**

DE'KARI

TRIGGADALE I II

Elijah R. Freeman

GOD BLESS THE TRAPPERS I, II, III

THESE SCANDALOUS STREETS I, II, III

FEAR MY GANGSTA I, II, III

THESE STREETS DON'T LOVE NOBODY I, II

BURY ME A G I, II, III, IV, V

A GANGSTA'S EMPIRE I, II, III, IV

THE DOPEMAN'S BODYGAURD

Tranay Adams

THE STREETS ARE CALLING

Duquie Wilson

MARRIED TO A BOSS... I II

By Destiny Skai & Chris Green

KINGZ OF THE GAME I II III

Playa Ray

SLAUGHTER GANG I II

By Willie Slaughter

THE HEART OF A SAVAGE

By Jibril Williams

FUK SHYT

By Blakk Diamond

DON'T F#CK WITH MY HEART I II

By Linnea

ADDICTED TO THE DRAMA I II

By Jamila

<u>BOOKS BY LDP'S CEO, CA$H</u>

<u>TRUST IN NO MAN</u>

<u>TRUST IN NO MAN 2</u>

<u>TRUST IN NO MAN 3</u>

<u>BONDED BY BLOOD</u>

<u>SHORTY GOT A THUG</u>

<u>THUGS CRY</u>

<u>THUGS CRY 2</u>

<u>THUGS CRY 3</u>

<u>TRUST NO BITCH</u>

<u>TRUST NO BITCH 2</u>

<u>TRUST NO BITCH 3</u>

<u>TIL MY CASKET DROPS</u>

<u>RESTRAINING ORDER</u>

<u>RESTRAINING ORDER 2</u>

<u>IN LOVE WITH A CONVICT</u>

<u>Coming Soon</u>

BONDED BY BLOOD 2

BOW DOWN TO MY GANGSTA

Heartless Goon

CPSIA information can be obtained
at www.ICGtesting.com
Printed in the USA
LVHW011746121119
637142LV00013B/440